HER CHRISTMAS RODEO COWBOY

BIG SKY CHRISTMAS BOOK 2

JENNA HENDRICKS

J.L. HENDRICKS

This book is a work of fiction. All of the characters, organizations, and events portrayed in this novel are either products of the author's imagination or are used fictitiously.

Cover Design by Victoria Cooper

First Edition November 2020

TABLE OF CONTENTS

BOOKS BY JENNA HENDRICKS

Triple J Ranch –

Book 0 - Finding Love in Montana (Join my newsletter to get this book for free)

Book 1 - Second Chance Ranch – also available on audio

Book 2 – Cowboy Ranch

Book 3 – Runaway Cowgirl Bride

Book 4 – Faith of A Cowboy

Book 5 – TBD

Book 6 – TBD

Big Sky Christmas –

Book 1 – Her Montana Christmas Cowboy

Book 2 – Her Christmas Rodeo Cowboy

See these titles and more: https://JennaHendricks.com

OTHER BOOKS BY J.L. HENDRICKS (MY 1ST PEN NAME)

New Orleans Magic

Book 0.5: Magic's Not Real

Book 1: New Orleans Magic

Book 2: Hurricane of Magic

Book 3: Council of Magic

Worlds Away Series

Book 0: Worlds Revealed (join my Newsletter to get this exclusive freebie)

Book 1: Worlds Away

Book 2: Worlds Collide

Book 2.5: Worlds Explode

Book 3: Worlds Entwined

A Shifter Christmas Romance Series

Book 0: Santa Meets Mrs. Claus

Book 1: Miss Claus and the Secret Santa

Book 2: Miss Claus under the Mistletoe

Book 3: Miss Claus and the Christmas Wedding

Book 4: Miss Claus and Her Polar Opposite

The FBI Dragon Chronicles

Book 1: A Ritual of Fire

Book 2: A Ritual of Death

Book 3: A Ritual of Conquest

See these titles and more at https://www.jlhendricksauthor.com/

NEWSLETTER SIGN-UP

By signing up for my newsletter, you will get a free copy of the prequel to the Triple J Ranch series, Finding Love in Montana. As well as another free book from J.L. Hendricks.

If you want to make sure you hear about the latest and greatest, sign up for my newsletter at: Subscribe to Jenna Hendricks' newsletter. I will only send out a few e-mails a month. I'll do cover reveals, snippets of new books, and give-aways or promos in the newsletter, some of which will only be available to newsletter subscribers.

JENNA HENDRICKS
Finding Love in Montana
A Triple J Ranch Prequel

PROLOGUE

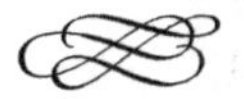

With the sun shining and his fishing pole in hand, Cove Hamilton went down to the creek to join his friend, Sam Keith, at their favorite fishing spot on the last day of summer.

"Hey, you can't be here. This's our spot," Sam said to a little girl with strawberry blonde hair in pigtails and a cute button nose.

"This is public property. I can be here if I want to." The little eight-year-old girl pouted and crossed her arms over her chest. She had two other girls standing beside her doing the same thing.

"Nuh-uh! I claimed this spot earlier this summer." Sam had been there almost every day that summer with his best friend, Cove, to fish and horse around until it was time to go home and do more chores. He was *not* about to let some stinky girls ruin his last day of summer and try to steal his spot, or scare away the fish. Not that they had had much luck fishing that summer. But he didn't care. All that mattered was fishing with his best buddy before school started back up on Monday.

"No way! We claimed this spot before school was even out last year," Betty-Sue Peterson exclaimed. Her light-brown ponytail bobbed behind her as she nodded her head enthusiastically.

"That's right," Elizabeth Beacon agreed. She narrowed her eyes when Cove walked up and stood next to Sam.

"Hi-ya. Whatcha doing?" Cove smiled, and all three girls returned his smile and uncrossed their arms. Cove had always had a way with the opposite sex, even at the ripe old age of eight. His casual demeanor and sweet white smile worked wonders on girls, and later on, women.

"We're swimming, of course. It *is* the last day of summer." Lottie Summers looked at Cove and rolled her eyes.

Cove chuckled and waved them over. "Please, be our guest."

"Cove!" Sam whined. "It's our spot. They'll scare the fish away."

"What fish?" Lottie asked. "Aren't they in the other stream, on the other side of Mr. Fisher's land?"

"No, nope. Totally wrong. You need to go over there and swim in that river." Sam pointed in the direction Lottie had mentioned.

"Come on, let the girls swim." Cove watched Lottie, and his little heart beat faster. *I'm gonna marry that girl when we grow up.*

Sam pulled on Lottie's pigtails then ran upstream so he and Cove could start fishing before the girls could scare them away.

Lottie stuck her tongue out at Sam. "You're just a rude little boy, Samuel Keith! I hope you fall in and scare the fish away for good."

Her friends joined her and stuck their tongues out at Sam's back while he ran away.

Cove smiled and nodded his head. "Enjoy your swim, Miss Lottie."

He never got his wish. Instead, he was the best man to his best friend when Sam married Lottie Summers after they graduated from high school.

CHAPTER 1

TWENTY-TWO YEARS LATER…

Even after all these years, Cove Hamilton never forgot Lottie Summers. Well, now she went by Lottie Keith.

Before Cove could get up the nerve to ask out the prettiest girl in junior high, his best friend Sam Keith did. When she said yes, it broke Cove's heart.

His heart broke again when his best friend and rodeo buddy died during a show. He was gored by the bull he was riding and left behind his wife and baby girl.

With Sam's dying breath, he said, "Take care of them. I know you've loved Lottie our whole lives." He coughed up blood.

"No, Sam. You're going to make it." Not caring that tears ran down his cheeks, Cove held his best friend's hand and prayed that God wouldn't take him.

"It's alright, you're what they need now." Sam didn't say anything else. He left this plane of existence on the way to the hospital, and Lottie never got to say goodbye to the man she'd loved since she was only thirteen years old.

Cove stood outside the Frenchtown Roasting Company and wiped the lone tear from his cheek. He hadn't thought about Sam's last words in many years. His best friend died seven years ago, but it still hurt to think about that final day.

He had kept his promise to Sam, and whenever he was in town he checked in on Lottie and Quinn, Sam's little girl. Only she wasn't so little anymore. She had turned eight a couple months back, and he sent her several gifts and a long letter apologizing for not being there on her special day. It was the first one he had missed. He hated doing it, but he thought he had to win that rodeo.

While Cove also rode bulls, he hadn't had the level of success Sam did until his best friend was gone. Part of him felt guilty for taking his buddy's place in the rodeo line-up, his sponsors, and even the love of his daughter. But he knew that Sam would have wanted it that way. They'd had several conversations about what to do if one of them died. Bull riding was one of the most dangerous sports out there, and they both knew what they had signed up for.

Over the years, Cove had won many belt buckles and saddles, and even two finals in Vegas. Every time he won, he wished Sam was there with him to celebrate. When he came home for visits, Quinn was always the one who wanted to see the buckles or saddles, and celebrated with him. Lottie…she wanted nothing to do with rodeo cowboys.

Now, Cove wished he would have come home for Quinn's birthday. It didn't matter that he had won that rodeo. His season was now over. He hadn't won another one after that, and continued to drop in the rankings until he was cut from the finals.

Looking in the window of Frenchtown Roasting Company, his heart soared when he saw Quinn sitting in the back with the new girl in town. Cove hadn't seen Lottie yet, but he knew she was in there. She was never far from her little girl.

A huge smile spread across his face when he watched Lottie walk in from the back and smile at a customer.

He was home.

* * *

When he finally got up the nerve to walk inside, he was assailed by the sights, sounds, and scents of Christmas. Cove knew how much Lottie loved Christmas. She had always gone overboard, even when they were kids. In fact, Lottie wore ugly Christmas sweaters before they became a thing. She just thought they were cute and whimsical, or something like that. He was pretty sure that was what caught Sam's attention in the eighth grade.

That Christmas was when Sam had started telling Cove what a pretty girl Lottie was, instead of complaining that she always interrupted their time fishing. Or wanted to get a game of boys versus girls together for softball instead of letting the boys play baseball. Sam had always thought, up until that year, that girls should be cheerleaders, not players. But after that Christmas, Sam was usually the first to join her softball games.

When Cove's senses went into Christmas overdrive, he felt a thud against his legs and looked down to find Quinn hugging him. "Princess Quinnie. I've missed you."

"I've missed you, Uncle Cove." She hugged him harder.

He wasn't exactly her uncle. Since he wasn't related to Sam, he wasn't related to Quinn. But he had been there when she was born and for almost all the major milestones in her life. And he loved it when she called him *uncle*.

"What did you bring me this time?" The little girl pulled back and smiled adoringly up into the face of the cowboy she had wrapped around her little finger.

Cove smiled at Quinn. "What makes you think I brought you anything?" He raised a brow.

With a dramatic eye roll and toss of her arms, Quinn responded, "Because you alllllways bring me gifts." She narrowed her eyes and put her little hands on her tiny hips. "Now, you didn't forget, did you Uncle Cove?"

Lottie stifled a laugh.

Cove chuckled. "Precocious little queenie, aren't you?" He patted Quinn's cheek.

The little princess backed up. "I'm not preco..co..toos." She tossed her blonde locks behind her back. "I'm pretty."

With a smile the size of Montana, Cove said, "Of course you are."

Quinn clapped her hands and beamed. "So?"

"Oh, you want a present, don't you?" Cove looked stern and put a hand on his heart. "I'm sorry, but I think the only presents I brought you aren't ready for you to open yet."

The little girl frowned. "What's that mean?"

"It means"—Lottie pointed a finger at her daughter—"that you shouldn't be asking anyone for gifts, even Uncle Cove. It's not a *gift* when you demand it."

Quinn's little bottom lip protruded, and she blinked rapidly.

"Oh, be still my beating heart." Cove looked to Lottie. "Your little girl is going to have every male, no matter their age, from here to Timbuktu wrapped around her little finger within the next year, two years tops."

Lottie sighed. "I know." She shook her head and smiled proudly. "I don't know what I'm going to do once she turns sixteen."

"Sixteen? I think you're gonna need to carry around a shotgun when she turns twelve. Those little boys aren't gonna know what hit 'em the second they *notice* her."

"Now don't go borrowing trouble. She's just barely eight years old. I have a long time to go before we need to worry about boys." Lottie pursed her lips and clucked her tongue.

Cove put his hands in the air. "Hey now, I just think you might want to start thinking about getting yourself a man soon. Someone who will love Quinn like a daughter and help shoo away those pesky boys. That's all."

"Now I know you've gone crazy. Did a bull dump you on your head, Cove Hamilton? How many times do I gotta tell you, I'm not ever marrying again." Lottie turned around and headed to the back room, grumbling to herself about not needing a man, nor wanting one.

"What did I say?" Cove turned confused eyes to Quinn and shrugged his shoulders.

"I think Momma needs a man."

Quinn sounded way too grown up for Cove's heart, and he gulped. "We might want to keep that between us," Cove whispered.

"Oh, I don't know. I think that might be a request for Santa to help fill." The jolly ol' man whom the entire town referred to as Santa Claus during the Christmas season smiled at Quinn and shook hands with Cove. "Cove, it's good to have you home again. How long are you here for?"

Santa's wife, affectionately known as Mrs. Claus, but who was really Jessica Lambton, smiled and leaned down to hug Quinn. "Have you asked Santa for a husband for your mommy?"

The little girl's eyes widened, and she squealed. "Not yet." She turned to Christopher Lambton, AKA Santa Claus, and asked, "Santa, when can I tell you what I want for Christmas? I already know." She clapped her hands and bounced on the balls of her feet.

"Ho, ho, ho. I think now is as good a time as any. Why

don't you come join me at a table and sit on my lap?" Santa led little Quinn over to a clean table and sat down in a chair.

He put her on his lap, and she leaned in to whisper in his ear. "I want a daddy and a baby brother for Christmas."

Not surprised by the first item, but shocked by the second, Santa leaned back in his chair and thought for a moment. "Do you know long it takes to make a baby?"

With wide eyes, Quinn nodded. "Mmhm. Mrs. Anderson at school had a baby boy last year, and she said it took nine months to cook it up in her oven."

Santa chuckled. "Yes, but she also has a husband, doesn't she? Do you think that a mommy should have the daddy before she *cooks* up a baby?"

Again, the girl nodded enthusiastically. "Of course. It's better if there is a daddy. Can I get a daddy this Christmas? Then next Christmas, a baby brother?"

Santa looked to Cove, and then down to Quinn. "Do you have someone in mind to be your new daddy?"

Little hands went up to cover the cute lilting sounds of Quinn's laugh. "I do."

"I see. And do you think he wants to be your daddy?" Santa thought he might, but before he meddled in the affairs of another man's heart, he needed to make sure. Her enthusiastic nod had Santa laughing heartily. "I'll see what I can do. I might need the help of Mrs. Claus on this one."

"I can help too, Santa."

Her earnest eyes melted his heart, and he hugged little Quinn. "I bet you can."

CHAPTER 2

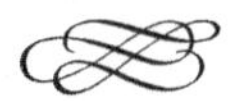

Lottie was so grateful it was Thanksgiving morning. For the first time in a very long time, she slept in until after seven and lazed in bed for a while before getting up and making herself a cup of coffee. She was going to let her little girl sleep in, too.

Cove had been spending a lot of time with them lately, and she was confused as to why he was still hanging around. Usually when he came home for a visit it was only for a few days. Even if there weren't any rodeos for him to perform in, he still never stayed long. She was going to have to ask him why he was still there and how long he planned on staying.

The last thing Lottie needed was Quinn getting her little heart broken when Cove left for the next rodeo. The past two years, whenever Cove left, Quinn was sad for a few days. And when Quinn was sad, Lottie was sad.

As she prepared her coffee, she checked her phone for a message from her best friend, Chloe. Last night she had gotten stuck in a snowstorm on her way home for the holiday weekend, but she still hadn't heard from her friend. She also hadn't heard from Brandon.

Now that would be a great couple. As she sat there sipping her coffee, she planned out how she was going to get those two crazy kids together. She, along with the rest of the town, was completely shocked and disappointed when Brandon left town a year ago and broke up with Chloe. Now that he was back for good, she hoped he would pick up where he left off.

Chloe might say she wasn't interested, but Lottie could tell that whenever Brandon was near her friend would get a sparkle in her eyes. It was time the two of them recognized their feelings for each other and made that leap of faith.

Her own love life, or lack thereof, had nothing to do with Lottie wanting to make sure that Chloe and Brandon finally got together and stayed together. Nope, she just wanted to see her friends happy. It didn't matter if she couldn't be happy, she still wanted everyone else around her to be full of joy and get exactly what God had planned for them.

Losing her husband at such a young age, and with a baby, had turned Lottie off of all men. Especially men who rode in the rodeo. Since her husband Sam died seven years ago, she had not had one date, nor did she want one. Everyone told her eventually she would want to date again. She was too young to stay a widow the rest of her life. But she would show them.

Seeing the news coverage of how her husband had died just about killed her. If she hadn't had Quinn, she didn't know if she would have made it. The good Lord must have known what was coming and gave her Quinn to help get her through the most difficult thing a wife would ever have to do—bury her own husband.

Thank you, Lord, for my little girl. I know I don't say it enough, but I am truly grateful for her. Please give me the strength to raise her the way You would want me to. And to keep up with her.

Lottie thought about what Cove had said the day he returned, and she cringed. There was no way she needed a man to help her take care of Quinn. She had her own shotgun and could do just as good a job of scaring away the boys, and eventually the men, who would hound her beautiful daughter.

Her beautiful daughter. Lottie sighed and wished Sam was here to see her. He would be just as entranced by his little girl as Cove was. The rodeo star did treat her little girl with love and care, just like an uncle should. However, Lottie wondered if it was smart to let Quinn get so close to someone who wasn't really family. Would she get her little heart broken if something happened to Cove like it did her daddy? No, she could never try to get between their sweet relationship.

All little girls did need a daddy figure. And last year when she had her first daddy-daughter dance, Cove had come home to take her to it. Lottie cried when they left, but she was truly grateful to Cove for stepping in where Sam couldn't.

Sam, I hope you're up there watching over our little girl and approve of Cove. They had never spoken about what would happen if he died young, so she had to wing it when the worst happened. And she thought she had done a great job, so far.

One thing Cove had said was accurate: the boys would swamp her daughter. Quinn was so outgoing and sweet, not to mention beautiful, that even now little boys and girls always wanted to be her friend. As long as her little girl stayed down to earth, she would always have friends.

"Momma?" Quinn rubbed her eyes as she walked into the kitchen and sat on her mom's lap.

"Hey, little girl. Happy Thanksgiving." Lottie kissed her daughter's head.

Quinn turned her head up to her mommy and puckered

her lips for a better kiss. Lottie was happy to oblige. "Happy Thanksgiving, Momma."

The sleepy tone of Quinn's eight-year-old voice caused Lottie to hug her daughter tight and smile. It was mornings like this that kept Lottie going. She lived for her daughter. Everything she did was to ensure that Quinn had the best life she possibly could.

"Today we're going to have two Thanksgiving dinners! So, do you want a small breakfast?" With Cove in town, they had been invited to the Hamiltons as well as her own parents' house for traditional meals. They would end the day with her folks on their ranch outside of town and start at noon with Cove and his family on their ranch, which were at opposite ends of the valley.

"I want cereal." Quinn got off her momma's lap and went to get her own bowl and spoon. It was a princess pink bowl with a matching spoon. The end of the spoon had a gold crown that had seen better days. The gold had been almost worn off from being used just about every day.

Lottie stood up, pulled down two boxes of cereal, and got out the milk. "Ok, which one do you want?" She held up a box of Cinnamon Toast Crunch cereal and a box of Lucky Charms.

Quinn pointed to the Cinnamon Toast Crunch.

"My favorite, too." Lottie kissed the top of her daughter's head before pouring her a bowl.

"Can I stay the night with Grammy and Poppy?" Quinn ate her breakfast without even looking up.

"You don't want to work the shop with me tomorrow?" It was Black Friday, and Lottie would be in extra early to get things open for those shoppers who would head over to Missoula for the crazy Christmas shopping before the crack of dawn. Just like for the stores, it was a fantastic day for sales for her shop, too.

Quinn scrunched her nose. "Are you kiddin'? I wanna sleep in."

Lottie chuckled. Her little girl liked to sleep, but she also loved being in the shop with her. She hoped this wasn't a sign of what was to come in just a few short years when she went through puberty. "Do you want to come over at all tomorrow?"

The little girl looked up from her cereal bowl and tilted her head. "I think I want to come visit in the afternoon, when there will be more kids to play with."

"Ah, I see." So, it wasn't really all about sleeping in, it was about who she could play with. She must have remembered last year, when there were zero kids with the moms who came in early to get their caffeine jolts before Christmas shopping. It made much more sense. "Alright, if Grammy and Poppy don't mind bringing you in tomorrow afternoon, that'll be fine."

Quinn jumped up and spilled her bowl of cereal in the process. "Yeah! I get to play with the new colt, too!"

It was all starting to make more sense. Lottie went to the sink and grabbed the dishcloth to clean up the mess. "Why don't you go and take a shower and pack for the night? You can use your new purple princess suitcase Cove sent you for your birthday."

"Yeah!" The girl had all the energy in world. She ran to her room to gather clothes for her shower and got herself ready as Lottie cleaned the kitchen and prepared herself for a long day.

Before she left for Cove's house, she texted her friend to see if she was home safely. With no response, she texted Brandon. While she was texting, a message from him came in. *Chloe's fine. She had to stop at a diner along the way for most of the night, but she's home and napping.*

Lottie backed out of what she was going to type and instead wrote, *Thank goodness. Thanks for letting me know.* With her friend home safely, Lottie could enjoy the rest of the day and not worry about Chloe. She would call her friend after her first dinner, on her way to her parents' place.

When they pulled up to the Hamilton ranch, Cove was already outside waiting for them.

Lottie got out of her SUV and went to help Quinn, but Cove was already there. "Hey, cowboy. Happy Thanksgiving."

Cove smiled at Lottie as Quinn hugged him. "Happy Thanksgiving to the both of you."

"I wasn't sure what to bring, so I brought fresh pumpkin pie and apple pie." Lottie went to the back and pulled out a covered box that smelled like a bakery.

"Oh, please tell me you did the crumbles on top like I like?" Cove licked his lips and rubbed his cold hands together.

"Is there any other way?" Lottie laughed, and Cove took the box from her and led them all inside.

Cove lived with his brother and sister-in-law on their ranch when he was home. It was the Hamilton family ranch. Their parents retired and moved to Boca Raton a couple years back. They only came to visit in the summer and for a week at Christmas. Lottie remembered that Mr. Hamilton had rheumatoid arthritis, and his doctor had suggested a warmer climate might help him with his pain levels. As far as she knew, it did.

"Did you hear from your parents yet?" Lottie asked as Cove helped her off with her big winter jacket.

Quinn had already thrown her winter gear down on the

ground and was running around, looking to see who all was there.

"I did. They called first thing this morning. They're having a big turkey dinner at the club today with all of their friends. Then they're going golfing." He snorted. "Did you ever see my dad as a golfer?"

Mr. Hamilton was a big and burly man. He had always worn a long, thick beard and was a bit gruff. When Lottie was growing up, she always compared him to those guys in ZZ Top. Sam and Cove had agreed with her.

"I still can't believe he joined a golf club and shaved his beard. But your mom, I'll bet she's totally in her element. She never did seem to be like the other ranch moms." When Lottie would come around as a kid, Mrs. Hamilton always wore skirts or dress slacks with sweater sets and a pearl necklace. Lottie thought Cove's mom should have been in a country club, not a cattle ranch.

Cove chuckled. "Yes, she is. The last time I visited, she looked radiant. I don't think I'd ever seen her so happy. I think it was the best thing the both of them could have done. Even my dad is happier now than he was."

"Do you think it's because of the weather?" Lottie had always wondered about the gruffness of Cove's dad. But if he was as happy as Cove seemed to think, maybe the old adage was true? *A happy wife makes a happy house?* That was something she wouldn't know, since she hadn't had much experience being a wife.

"Lottie, it's good to see you. And thank you for bringing pie today." Cove's sister-in-law, Alice Hamilton, sniffed and smiled from ear to ear.

Lottie leaned in for a hug. "Thank you for inviting us."

Lottie had known Alice when they were kids, but since she was five years older, they had never been close.

Although, the past few years they had gotten close, since Cove always invited Lottie and Quinn over to the family ranch when he was in town. And she loved Quinn as though she were her niece.

"Are you kidding me? You're always invited." Alice beamed.

"And if you want to bring some of your baked goods, we won't complain," Duke Hamilton, Cove's big brother, joked and patted his stomach.

"Oh, I see how it is. I'm only invited for my baking skills, huh?" Lottie snorted and leaned in to hug Duke.

Alice play-slapped her husband's arm. "Now Duke Hamilton, you be nice. It's rare to have other women in the house. So don't go ruining this for me." Alice had three rambunctious boys. She'd always wanted a girl, but the good Lord had never seen fit to give her one. While she wasn't too old to still have kids, she was only thirty-five after all, her youngest was already seven, and she had not been blessed with any more kids since.

"Don't worry." Lottie waved a hand. "I know that the way to a man's heart is through his stomach. And I have no problems with bringing baked goods whenever I visit." She laughed. "And any time you want to get away from all this testosterone, you just come into town and visit me. I'm sure Quinn will love to pull out her tea set for you as well."

Since Alice only had boys, she played tea with Quinn whenever she got the chance. "I actually have a new tea set for Quinn to try out today. You're welcome to join us, if you like?"

"Thank you, I think I might do that." Lottie didn't get to have traditional tea too often, and enjoyed the tea parties with her daughter when they had time. Plus, she really liked Alice.

The day went by smoothly, except for when Lottie caught

Cove looking at her funny. When they sat down to dinner an hour after she arrived, she was seated next to Cove, and Quinn was on his other side. Lottie got the feeling they were put together as though they were a family, even though they most certainly weren't.

There were three other couples there, which might explain why they were seated as they were. On the other side of Quinn were the Johnsons and their little girl, who was a year older than Quinn.

The Hamilton boys, who were too rowdy and rambunctious for a formal meal, were seated at the kids' table with the Lowrys' two boys.

Across from Lottie and Cove sat Mr. and Mrs. Lambton, affectionately known as the town's royal couple, or Santa and Mrs. Claus. While they technically didn't don their Christmas outfits until the day after Thanksgiving, everyone began calling them Santa and Mrs. Claus once Christmas decorations started showing up around town. Which tended to coincide with the snow. And since they'd had snow for a few weeks now, the Lambtons were now called the Clauses.

Next to the Lambtons sat Mr. and Mrs. Lowry with their two teenaged daughters, who did know how to sit at a formal table, unlike their younger brothers who had been relegated to the kids' table.

It was a great and lively group of neighbors and friends. Conversation flowed freely, but so did the knowing looks everyone kept giving Lottie. When she turned to ask Cove about it, she noticed the way he looked at her. It *wasn't* like a friend would. She grew antsy in her seat and worried people might get the wrong idea. And if gossip spread about them, it would make its way back to Quinn. The last thing she wanted was to hurt her baby girl.

"Cove," she whispered, "why is everyone staring?"

He cleared his throat and looked around. For the first time that day, Cove realized that people were looking at him funny. Did they know how he felt about Lottie? Surely no one except his brother knew. And his brother would never tell a soul that he had been in love with Lottie Summers, now Lottie Keith, since they were only eight years old. Hoping to take the limelight off himself and Lottie, he turned to Santa. "So, Santa, how's the *list* coming this year?"

Santa took his cloth napkin off his lap and wiped his mouth and beard clear of any crumbs from the stuffing he might have left behind. "I'm pleasantly surprised by how many little boys and girls have been good this year." His eyes twinkled when he turned to Quinn. "In fact, I think I'm going to be able to deliver on all the *special* gifts that the extra-good little *girls*, and boys, have requested." He hoped Quinn understood what he was trying to tell her.

Cove picked up on the fact that Santa was trying to give Quinn a message, but he had no clue what the jolly ol' man was saying to his favorite little girl. Special gift? Cove would have to ask Santa what that was and how he could help ensure she got what she wanted. The little blonde angel next to him was exceptionally well behaved that year and deserved everything she wanted. Cove had put aside extra money this year and would see to it that Quinn had the best Christmas yet.

"I saw the ornaments that will be going up next week on the town tree. There's a lot of need this year." Lottie looked at Santa and Mrs. Claus, who smiled in return.

"Yes, there certainly is. But I think our town has already started to see to it everyone will have a wonderful Christmas." Mrs. Claus took a sip of her coffee. "I spoke with Chloe Manning the other day, and she had some wonderful ideas of how to help some of our children who could use a little extra this year."

Cove furrowed his brow. "Do we have some families having a tough time of it? I mean, more than normal?" He hadn't been home in a while, which was one reason why he had decided to stay at least through the new year and maybe even longer. He missed his hometown and the people he'd grown up with. Plus, this was the first year he hadn't made it into the finals in ten years. His body needed the rest.

Santa put his fork down before he could take another bite and sighed. "Sadly, we do. There are a few families who are struggling more than usual. The drought this past year has affected several ranches and farms, those who don't have access to their own wells and rely on the little lakes and creeks that normally run through their land."

"So, water is an issue again? But haven't we already started off on a great foot with snow this year?" The blizzard that came through last night almost cancelled their Thanksgiving dinner plans that day. Thankfully, they worked with their neighbors and were able to plow the small road leading up to their ranch from the main highway, since the county most likely would not have gotten to it that day.

Usually after a major storm like what they'd had, only the main highways and the streets in town were plowed on day one. The rest would get taken care of over the next few days. Which was why so many ranchers and farmers had small plows of their own that they could attach to their four-wheel-drive trucks, or tractors. Neighbors helped neighbors around these parts.

"One blizzard does not make the season," Duke reminded Cove.

"True." Cove nodded. "But it can signal that it will be a snowy season, right?" He looked around the table at the wizened older men who had seen their fair share of good and bad seasons.

Mr. Johnson spoke up. "I think we'll see a wet and cold winter this year. My ash and beech trees turned early, and were brighter than normal. Plus, have you seen all the geese already gone south? I think it was in record numbers this year."

The Johnson family had always trusted old wives' tales and the *Farmers' Almanac* more than any weather station, and was almost always on target. So, when he forecasted a cold and wet winter, Cove believed the man.

Santa nodded. "Yes, my arthritis is really kicking in early this year, and worse than usual. I do think we'll get plenty of snowpack to help with planting season come spring. But, that doesn't mean folks will make it through this winter without a little extra help."

Cove thought about what everyone was saying. While he did have plenty of money put aside for his retirement, which might be coming sooner than expected, he also wanted to help his neighbors and friends this year. God had blessed him with a career that helped to make him wealthy. He would pull out some of that blessing and share with others this Christmas. He was already planning what he would do on Monday night at the town's Christmas tree-lighting event.

After their early dinner, Lottie helped to serve up her pies for dessert. When she sat back down, her knee grazed Cove's thigh. Heat pulsed through him, and he looked at her.

Lottie felt the warmth of the cowboy next to her when she sat down and realized her chair had been moved closer to his. Whether by design or accident, she didn't know. But it caused heat to flare up her neck, and she turned her face down and moved her knee away from him. "Sorry about that."

"I'm not." Cove's hand grazed hers before she pulled it back and cleared her throat.

"So"—Lottie's shaky voice caused Cove to chuckle under his breath—"what's everyone's plans for the rest of the day?"

In unison, the men all called out, "Football!"

The women laughed, and Alice asked Quinn if she was ready for a tea party.

Lottie decided that was the best thing for her, as it would get her far away from Cove. There was something strange going on, and she didn't want to find out what it was, either. Awkwardness was the last thing she needed in her life. It was complicated as it was with Christmas and all the events she was going to host or participate in this season. There wasn't one week from here on out when she didn't have at least two events going on, in addition to running her store.

With all the events going on, her regular part-time staff was going to be working full-time, and she would be putting in more overtime than she could count. Thank goodness Cove was going to be around for a while.

Wait, did she just think that? Was she truly glad Cove would be home through Christmas? Or was it just so she would have an easy babysitter? She must be more tired than she realized.

When they said their goodbyes an hour later, Cove walked Lottie and Quinn out to her SUV.

"Uncle Cove, when will I see you again?" Quinn pouted and hung onto Cove's hand.

"Oh, honey. Don't worry. I'm not leaving any time soon. I'll be at the town Thanksgiving dinner on Saturday, so I'll see you then, alright?" He leaned down and bussed her little cheek with a loud raspberry.

She giggled. "Alright. And will you sit with us in church on Sunday?"

Cove tickled her sides, and she wiggled around giggling. "Of course, I love sitting in church with you."

Quinn hugged him again and got inside the car and fastened her booster seat.

"Thank you for today. I know Quinn loves spending time with you and your family." Lottie was about to get in her car when Cove pulled her toward him for a hug as well.

At first, she was shocked. They didn't normally hug. But his warmth pulled her in, and she wrapped her arms around his waist and set her head on his shoulder. It had been a long time since a man hugged her like this. Sure, she got the occasional side-hug from friends at church, but a full-blown, arms-wrapped-around-her-and-held-tight kinda hug was rare.

In fact, it was so rare she had forgotten how good it felt. Not realizing what she had done, she sighed.

Cove hadn't planned on pulling Lottie in for a tight hug. It was something he just did. But oh garland, was he glad he did. With her head on his shoulder and her arms around his waist, he was in heaven. Something inside him told him this was his Christmas. He was finally going to go after the woman he'd wanted his whole life, and she would allow him to court her.

When Quinn giggled, it broke the mood and Cove felt Lottie pull away from him, not just physically, but emotionally as well.

"Well, thank you again." She averted her gaze and quickly got in her SUV.

Cove watched them pull away and hoped he hadn't messed things up already.

CHAPTER 3

Three in the morning came very early for Lottie. She hadn't slept well, even though she didn't stay long with her parents. Cove's scent was all over her when she got home, and since she showered in the morning, it kept her up all night. He smelled like horse, leather, and cloves. It was a very alluring scent. Every time she fell asleep, she dreamt of Cove holding her like he did in his driveway.

In her dreams, she wanted him to kiss her. Then she kept hearing Quinn's giggle and it would wake her up. No matter what her dreams said, she did not want this complication. She and Cove had been childhood friends. He was her husband's best friend. She couldn't do that to Sam. It would break his heart if he knew she was with his best friend, wouldn't it?

No, she told herself over and over as she tried to go back to sleep. At two in the morning, she rolled over to where Sam used to sleep and put a hand on his pillow. When she pulled it toward her, she couldn't smell him anymore. His scent had melted away years earlier. In fact, she'd forgotten what he smelled like. Horses, for sure. All rodeo cowboys smelled like horses or bulls, no matter how much they showered. Did he have a leather scent as well? Then she would smell Cove on her, and she'd feel guilty for enjoying the way he held her and the way his scent enveloped her.

It was a good thing she owned a coffee shop. She was going to need a gallon of coffee and at least three pounds of sugar to keep her going on Black Friday.

When she showered, she scrubbed extra hard to get Cove off her. Then, when she smelled like her soap, she regretted removing any scent of Cove from her. His smell calmed her. He may have made her heart race, but he seemed to set the world to rights whenever he was near. She was so confused.

At least she would be so busy all day she wouldn't have time to think about him.

Or so she'd thought until he showed up in the afternoon with Quinn.

"Quinn, Cove. What are you two doing here?" Lottie wiped her hands on her red apron appliqued with a snowy Christmas scene.

"Your mom called, and she asked if I could pick up Quinn and bring her to you. Your dad needed help with a calf, and she couldn't leave." Cove sat at a table, and Quinn sat across from him.

"Thank you. That was very generous of you to help. Especially since her house must have been at least a two-hour drive in this weather." The previous night, it had taken Lottie almost two and a half hours to get to her mother's house since most of the side roads hadn't been plowed yet.

"No worries. I love spending time my little Quinnie." He mussed the little girl's hair, and she pushed his hand away without looking up from the picture she was coloring.

"Well, what can I get you?" Since she was already making her Christmas drinks and sweets, she figured he'd go for one of those.

"Large coffee and one of those cinnamon rolls, if you have any left?" His plain choice surprised Lottie.

"Actually, we do. Most people have ordered the Christmas specials today, so I still have an entire pan of cinnamon rolls." Lottie turned to her daughter. "How about you? Are you ready for lunch? I have a ham sandwich on a fresh croissant, just the way you like it."

Quinn scrunched her nose. "I already ate lunch. But I could make room for a cinnamon roll." She inclined her head and looked up through her lashes as though she were as innocent as an angel. And she probably was.

Cove reached across the table and mussed her hair. "How about I share mine with you?"

"That'll work. Quinn, I'll bring you a glass of milk, too." Lottie turned to walk away.

Her daughter yelled out, "Chocolate milk, please."

Shaking her head, Lottie didn't turn around but went to the back to get some chocolate milk for her daughter. She probably should have offered Cove something healthier so her daughter would have been more open to a healthier snack, but at least Cove was sharing instead of Quinn trying to eat a whole cinnamon roll herself. Since her rolls were one pound of sugar and carbs, this would work well, and she wouldn't have to worry about giving her daughter dessert after dinner that night.

"Hey." Cove came up behind Lottie while she was still in the back. "How about I take Quinn back to my ranch for the day while you work?"

"Really? You'd do that?" Lottie's wide eyes pricked with tears. She had planned on working all day and late into the night since Quinn was supposed to be staying all day long with Lottie's parents.

"You know how much I love Quinn. Plus, my family

adores her." Cove waited for Lottie's reply.

She nodded. "Alright, but be sure to bring her back here if she gets in your way, or if you need to do anything else. Or better yet, call me and I'll come get her." It would be about an hour each way for Lottie to do that, but it also meant she'd get in a lot of working hours without having to worry about Quinn that day.

"No worries." Cove took Quinn with him back to his family ranch for the day while Lottie continued to work like a Christmas elf.

Before she was done for the day, Lottie finally finished off her Christmas decorating of the store. That was cutting it too close for her. Inside, she had Christmas music playing and each table had its own decorations, helping her patrons to feel as though they were in a Christmas scene from Currier and Ives. There was real greenery everywhere she could put it up without having the fire department get on her case. She did have a fake tree that was up to fire code, and it was decorated with ornaments from specialty stores as well as Hallmark. There was candy cane-striped fancy ribbon woven throughout all the greenery. And she even had a few of the fake incandescent candles spread throughout the store.

Cove came back at the end of the day with Quinn, who was fast asleep in his arms with her head on his shoulder.

Lottie's nose burned, and she put a hand over her heart. They made such the perfect picture. It should have been Sam coming through the door with their daughter. But if it was going to be anyone else, she was glad it was Cove. Every day she saw him with her daughter, it began to feel more...right. She couldn't put words to it yet, but Cove truly was Quinn's uncle. No one else could have treated her so well, or loved her so much. Not even her actual uncle, who lived in California.

"She fell asleep in my truck when driving back to town. I didn't have the heart to wake her up." Cove held Quinn tightly in his arms and smiled at Lottie.

Lottie bit her lip. She didn't want to wake up Quinn. But she still had more work to do before she could leave.

"You still have more work to do, don't you?" Cove chortled.

"Yes." The only option was to put Quinn in her office and hope her daughter could sleep through the rest of the noise.

"How about I take her to your house and stay with her until you get home?" The cowboy held his hand out for Lottie's house keys.

"Are you sure you don't mind? It'll probably be at least another hour before I can get out of here." Not that Lottie wanted to keep working, but she had to. Their entire stock of pastries had been depleted that day, including the cinnamon rolls. She had to get a head start on dough for the next day or she'd start out behind.

"No worries. I think there's a replay of today's game that I missed anyway. I'll catch that while I wait for you."

With a nod and a smile, Lottie went to her office and pulled out her keys. After removing the house key from the ring, she went back out front and handed it to Cove. He pocketed the key and told Lottie he'd see her later.

When Lottie arrived home two hours later, she found not only Cove asleep on her couch in front of the TV, but also Quinn. And instead of a football game on TV, *It's A Wonderful Life* was finishing up. The tired mom shook her head and turned off the TV. She stood over the sleeping pair and smiled. What would it be like to come home to a husband who loved her daughter as though she was his own? Probably something like this.

When she realized where her tired mind was taking her,

she shook it off and grabbed two blankets. She covered them both up and went around turning off the lights. If her being there and making noise didn't wake either of them, then she was just going to let them sleep on the couch. They had both worn themselves out, obviously.

Lottie prayed that she'd get to sleep that night and not have a repeat of the previous night.

When she awoke to her alarm the next morning, she breathed a sigh of relief. Not once did she wake up during the night. Her exhaustion must have been enough to keep her asleep the entire night, including when a little monster came and joined her in bed.

Somehow, Quinn had climbed into her bed and taken all the blankets, while also turning to the side and putting her feet up against Lottie's legs. This wasn't the first time Lottie had woken up to her little girl sleeping in a strange position in her bed and hogging the covers, but it was the first time she had slept through it. Lottie must have really worn herself out the day before.

Thankfully, today would be a short day for her. Since everyone would be at the town's Thanksgiving dinner, she would close the shop up at three in the afternoon and come home for a shower and maybe even a quick nap if she was lucky. Her mom was coming over to watch Quinn that day, so she left Quinn in her bed when she got up to get ready for the morning.

Completely forgetting that Cove had slept on her couch, she walked out to find him still sleeping there and was so shocked, she yelped and jumped when he moved.

"What? What's wrong?" Cove jumped up and looked around with wide eyes as though there were a burglar in the house.

With a hand over her heart, she took in a few deep

breaths. "Sorry, I completely forgot you fell asleep and stayed over."

With a fuzzy head, Cove looked around and then down at the watch on his wrist. "What time is it?"

"Five a.m. I'm getting ready for work. Do you want some coffee?" Lottie headed toward the kitchen.

"Oh, little drummer boy! Sorry about that. I didn't intend to fall asleep last night." He looked around. "Where's Quinnie?"

"She's in my bed." Lottie chuckled and poured two cups of hot coffee that she had set to brew automatically. She handed a mug of black coffee to Cove, just the way he preferred it, and she put two creamers and a sugar in hers.

"Thanks. Mmm, this is good." Even at home she made good coffee. Cove doubted the woman ever made a bad cup of joe.

"I need to leave, and my mom's not here yet. Would you mind staying and keeping an ear out for Quinn until my mom arrives?" She hated asking him to do that, but if she didn't get going, her afternoon plans would be shot.

"Not a problem. In fact, I'd rather stay for a little bit longer as I wake up." His eyelids drooped, and he took a seat at her table as he sipped the hot brew.

"I take it you're no longer accustomed to early mornings?" Lottie had always gotten up before dawn. She was naturally a morning person, so this wasn't too difficult for her.

But Cove, he grew up on a ranch and had to get up early every day until he joined the rodeo. "Nope. When I left home, I stopped getting up so early. Usually I get up with the sun. And since it won't be up here for a few more hours, I'd normally still be asleep." He rubbed his eyes.

Lottie took another long drink of her coffee and transferred the rest to her travel mug. She filled it up and looked to Cove. "Ok, feel free to go back to sleep on the couch. My mom just texted—she won't be here until after six. I'll let her know you're here and not to worry." She only hoped her mom wouldn't get the wrong impression.

When Lottie left, Cove texted his brother to let him know he would be by soon to help with the chores. He said he fell asleep on a friend's couch.

Cove hoped no one would see his truck outside of Lottie's place and spread the word that he'd stayed over. In all the years he'd been home and helped out with Quinn, he'd never once spent the night. Not even by accident, like last night.

When Sarah Summers, Lottie's mom, came by, she was surprised to see him.

"Hi, Mrs. Summers. Didn't Lottie tell you I was helping out this morning?" He smiled when he stood up on the couch, which still held his messy covers from the night before.

When her eyes went from the mess on the couch to him, it dawned on him what she was seeing. He looked down and noticed his shirt was all rumpled. Then he scratched his chin and realized he hadn't shaved yet, and it was obvious. She must not have realized he had stayed the night until just then.

"I…um…yes. Lottie told me you were helping out this morning." And then, under her breath, "But I had no idea you stayed the night."

Cove's cheeks flushed. It wasn't like he had stayed the night *with* Lottie. He fell asleep on the couch with little Quinnie next to him. He ran a hand through his unruly hair. "Ah, yes. Well, I was over last night with Quinn and we fell asleep on the couch. I guess Lottie didn't want to wake me, soooo yeah." He winced when he saw the narrowed eyes of Lottie's mom boring a hole into him.

"I see. And where is my granddaughter now?" Sarah put her handbag on the entry table and looked around for Quinn.

"Um, I think at some point in the middle of the night she climbed into bed with Lottie. At least, that's what she said this morning when she asked if I could stay with Quinn until you got here." Cove was a grown man and didn't have to answer to anyone. But at the moment he felt like a little boy again, about to get scolded for staying out past curfew.

"Well," Sarah sniffed, "I'm here now. So you can go home and get cleaned up." She turned to go look in on Quinn. "And I hope I don't hear any rumors about you spending the night with my daughter." She arched an imperious brow at him before disappearing down the hall.

He let out a long sigh of relief. Without bothering to fold the blankets, he got his boots on, ran his hand through his hair a few times, and then headed home. The first thing he was going to do was take a long, hot shower. But his plans were put on hold when he arrived home to chaos.

A cow was having a tough time with labor, and his sister-in-law, Alice, told him he was needed in the barn.

"Duke, what's wrong?" Cove called out the moment he entered the barn and saw several long faces on the ranch's hands.

Mike, a cowboy who had worked on the ranch for as long as Cove could remember, shook his head. "It ain't lookin' good."

Some ranches could afford to lose a calf here and there, but their ranch couldn't. Not this year. Last year was a very lean year, and they didn't have many cows freshen. This year, they needed a strong, healthy lot of calves to help them get back on top. Losing one wouldn't hurt too much, but since it was the first of the winter season, it would send a bad signal to the ranch. A lot of the hands were superstitious, and if the first calf of the season didn't make it, it usually meant a bad season. They did not need anyone on the Hamilton ranch thinking it would be a bad year.

Sometimes, you could make your own back luck with thinking like that.

"How can I help?" Cove asked when he approached his brother and Steve Caruthers, the vet, in the birthing stall.

Steve looked up. "Come on in and hold this here cow. She's not doing well, and if she doesn't calm down I won't be able to help her."

Cove worked to keep the soon-to-be new momma down on her side. She didn't seem to want to stand, but she was anxious and kept moving and was very vocal about her pain. As a rancher, Cove had been present for too many births to count. But this one was different. Something about the cow and her situation spoke to him. His heart went out to her as she struggled with calving. "Is this her first?"

"Nope, it's her second. The first went smoothly." Duke pulled on the calf's front hooves when they made their way out of the birthing canal.

"You got it, Duke. That's it." The vet helped the ranch owner to deliver the calf while Cove held the cow's head and tried to soothe her by telling her a story of a little blonde princess who wanted to come and see her and her baby calf when they were up for a visit.

"Do you think she'll survive?" Cove looked at the calf that lay barely moving in front of its momma.

The vet sighed and shook his head. "I'm not rightly sure. All I can say is keep it warm and make sure its mom is fed and watered. The first seventy-two hours are vital. If she survives the first three days, then I think she'll have a good chance of making it."

"Got it. I'll keep an eye out on momma and baby when

I'm here, Duke. And help feed the calf if the momma rejects her." There was always the chance a cow would reject her calf, even if the calf could survive. Cove didn't understand why some cows, or animals of any sort, would reject their newborns. But it happened. And a good rancher always kept an eye out for his or her cattle. While Cove didn't own the ranch, it was his family ranch, and he'd be tarred and feathered before he willingly let anything happen to any of the animals on his ranch.

Once the momma seemed to take to her calf and the little female started suckling, they all stood up and left the pair to bond.

"I think they're going to be just fine." Cove patted Duke on the shoulder. "Should I call you poppa now?"

The men all laughed.

"If you call me poppa, we're gonna have words. I'm too young for that business." Duke shoved his little brother out the door into the cold white paddock before leading them all back to the house. "How about some hot coffee? And I'll see if Alice has any scones or danishes for us."

"That sounds like a plan. Thank you." The vet smiled and followed them into the house to warm up and fill his belly.

"So, I hear you spent the night with Lottie." Alice smirked and handed a cup of steaming-hot coffee to Cove.

"What?" Duke sputtered. "I thought you spent the night with a friend?" He narrowed his eyes at his little brother.

Cove put up his hands. "Whoa. It's nothing like that. Not at all. You know Lottie doesn't see me as anything more than Sam's best friend."

"Oh, I don't know. I think she might be changing her tune." Alice sat down next to her husband and took a sip of her coffee.

Cove shook his head. "Nope. She swore off rodeo

cowboys after Sam died. There's no way she'll ever look at me in *that* way."

Duke looked at his brother over the rim of his coffee mug. "Haven't you told her your plans?"

"What plans?" Alice asked.

"My little brother has finally decided it's time to settle down and stop riding bulls."

"Really? That's fantastic. Will you be moving in with us permanently?" Alice subconsciously touched her stomach.

"I..." Before Cove could finish, he noticed his sister-in-law's subtle tell. "I was thinking about getting myself a small spread nearby when some property came up. I don't know yet if I'm done. But my body is saying something different than my brain." He chuckled and rubbed his right knee.

Cove had taken quite a few falls this past year that caused a lot of pain. His doctor had told him it was probably time to retire. Combine that with his low ranks this past year, he knew it was time to at least think about it. But if Alice was expecting again, he couldn't stay there much longer. They would need his room for a new baby. And the Baker ranch wasn't ready for him to move into.

Mr. Baker wanted to spend some more time in the area and didn't want to sell until the new year, Cove knew because he had checked it out. He could get in one more year, couldn't he?

When Cove asked Mr. Baker why he put the ranch up for sale if he wasn't ready to move yet, the man answered, "Well, I thought it would take a long while for anyone to want my small spread. Can you give me a little time? Let's talk again after the new year."

When he stood up, his knee almost gave out on him, and he sat back down and had second thoughts again. Or was it more like fourth of fifth thoughts about retirement?

"Well, I know Lottie has been checking you out lately." Alice smiled. "She'd be crazy not to go for you. Especially if you were to retire."

"Maybe instead of getting a ranch, you could get a place in town and work with Lottie? I bet she'd be very happy to have your help in her store." Duke had wanted his brother to come home for the past few years. And he also thought Lottie would be a perfect addition to their family. Especially since he and his family already thought of Quinn as part of their lot.

"Whoa now, you're getting ahead of yourself." Cove shook his head, and an uncomfortable feeling stabbed him in the gut.

Steve looked on and laughed. "You know, your brother and sister are right. You and Lottie would be perfect together."

"Hey, now. I don't need no lip from the peanut gallery." Cove pointed a finger at the vet whom he'd known all his life. "You stay out of this."

CHAPTER 4

Later that day when Cove was all alone, he thought back to what everyone had said about him and Lottie and he smiled. Did Lottie really look at him *that* way? Did he stand a chance with the beautiful woman who had held his heart for as long as he could remember?

While out on the rodeo circuit, he had a reputation as a playboy. Not because he slept around or anything, but because he never went out on more than two or three dates with the same cowgirl. He had tried to get Lottie out of his heart and head, but he couldn't.

This past year, he even stayed away more than usual because of how he felt whenever he saw her. But now, when he heard what others were seeing from Lottie, well, hope started to bubble up in his chest. Maybe, just maybe he would have a chance with the love of his life if he retired now.

That afternoon was the town's annual Thanksgiving dinner. He always went with his family when he was in town. But this year, he'd have to try and sit with Lottie and Quinn. And he'd pay extra-close attention to how she looked at him. Cove thought back to that morning and realized she'd barely looked at him before she left for work. But he had spent the night on her couch, and she probably felt awkward about it all.

He only hoped the town wouldn't be gossiping about them. That was the last thing Lottie needed.

* * *

LOTTIE COULDN'T BELIEVE she had been so stupid as to let that rodeo cowboy sleep on her couch. It only took about an hour before the first customer came in and asked when she and Cove were getting married. When she turned confused eyes on Laura Anderson, the pretty brunette was only too happy to talk about the gossip that was already going around about her and Cove.

"It's nothing like that, and y'all know it. Why in the world would anyone think there's anything at all between me and Cove?" Lottie felt heat creeping up her neck, and she worried that Laura would think her blush meant she was guilty. She wasn't. The cowboy was important to her, sure. But he wasn't anything more than a close friend.

"Gracie was driving by your house this morning and saw Cove's truck outside. When he left your house, he looked all rumpled and unshaven." Laura's voice was getting louder the more excited she got talking about the possibility of Cove sleeping over at Lottie's.

"Now, Laura Anderson. You stop that right now!" Lottie pointed a finger at the gossipmonger in front of her. "You know very well that I swore off rodeo men when Sam died. In fact, I haven't even dated anyone since my husband." She crossed her arms over her chest and seethed. If she hadn't been so tired the night before, she wouldn't have let him sleep on her couch. She would have woken him up and sent him home. But she just didn't think. That would never happen again.

"But it's time, Lottie." Laura's expression changed from excited, gossiping mom to concerned friend. "Don't you think Sam would want you to be happy? And what about Quinn? She needs a daddy, don't you think?"

That was the last straw. Anger got the better of her, and Lottie pointed to the door. "Get out! The last thing I need is someone telling me what I need, or what my daughter needs. Especially someone who does nothing but go around town gossiping about her neighbors."

A collective gasp escaped everyone's lips, and the store was quieter than Lottie could ever remember, as the Christmas CDs that had been playing chose that moment to change over. When all eyes stared at Lottie, she turned tail and ran back to her office, praying she wouldn't cry in front of anyone. She was exhausted and confused—and Lord knew what else at that moment.

All Lottie wanted to do was go home and curl up in a ball and either cry or sleep. Maybe both? But she couldn't. She decided to give herself a few minutes to cry and then dry her tears and she'd start baking. At least that way, she wouldn't have to be out front where she could see anyone, or they could see her.

Not ten minutes after she'd wiped her face, she was mixing a batch of dough and her phone rang. "Hi, Chloe. It's good to hear from you."

Chloe Manning was Lottie's best friend who happened to be away this weekend, when she needed her the most.

"What's wrong? And don't tell me nothing. I know you, Lottie Keith. And I can hear the strain in your voice." The tone in Chloe's voice over the phone told Lottie she'd not stop until she got the entire story.

Lottie sighed. "You're right. Things are a mess. Or maybe it's just me? I don't know. But I do know that I need a friend right now."

"I wish I was there with you, Lottie. But can you tell me now over the phone?" Chloe's voice changed to that of a worried friend, and Lottie sank into a chair.

After a good long thirty-minute call, where Lottie got everything off her chest about the previous night and the gossipers, she began to feel better. She was going to have to apologize to Laura about her outburst. And not because the woman was a good customer—she was—but because it was the right thing to do. If Laura was at the Thanksgiving dinner later that day, she would do it then. She just wished the group of gossiping moms would give it a break.

* * *

LATER THAT DAY when she arrived at the town's community center for the Thanksgiving dinner, Lottie looked around for Laura. She just wanted to get this done and move on. Hopefully, word would get around that nothing happened and everyone would leave her alone. Especially since she had Quinn with her.

When Lottie couldn't find Laura, she decided to find a place to sit instead. Her mom waved her over, and the two of them joined her mother and father at a table along the side.

"Hi, Mom and Dad." Lottie kissed them both on the cheek, and Quinn gave them both big hugs.

"Quinnie, my girl." Michael Summers loved his little granddaughter and hugged her tightly.

Lottie knew her dad wanted her to move home with Quinn. It was never going to happen, and he understood that she needed to be in town, close to her shop, but it still didn't stop him from asking her on a semi-regular basis to move home. It had been a while since the last time he asked, and she would bet good money he'd be asking again soon. Especially if he heard the latest gossip about her.

The hair on the back of Lottie's neck stood on end, and she knew who was watching her. She cleared her throat and made sure there wasn't an empty seat next to her. She sat next to her father and put Quinn on her other side.

"Mr. and Mrs. Summers, it's good to see you both." He smiled his dazzling white smile at her parents and then turned liquid pools of gray onto her. "Lottie." His gaze lingered on her just a bit too long for comfort, and she squirmed in her seat.

Quinn jumped up. "Uncle Cove!" The exuberant little girl ran into Cove's outstretched arms and hugged his neck with her little arms.

"How's my little princess today?" Cove kissed her cheek and then spread little kisses down to her neck, where he blew a couple of raspberries and had her laughing and squirming in his arms.

"Uncle Cove," Quinn giggled, "stop it. That tickles." She squirmed and continued to laugh even after he stopped and put her down.

When Cove took the seat next to Lottie, he put Quinn in his lap and smiled at the people around his table. "I hope everyone had a wonderful Thanksgiving?"

Quinn put her hands on his face and forced him to look directly at her. "I did, Uncle Cove. Did you?" The little girl wanted his entire attention on her.

Cove was more than happy to oblige his little Quinnie. "I did. I had so much turkey, I think I gained at least a hundred pounds!"

Quinn giggled. "No you didn't."

"How do you know?" Cove kept his attention on Quinn, but out of the corner of his eye he noticed Lottie relaxing and even give a small smile.

"'Cause *I* don't even weigh that much." She leaned in and whispered, "Did you ask Santa for what you want this year? I did."

Cove whispered back, "What did you ask for?"

The little girl leaned back, and a frown covered her pretty little face. "I can't tell. You know that."

With wide eyes, he responded, "I do?"

Her little blonde head bobbed up and down. "Uh-huh. Everyone knows you can't tell what you asked Santa for, else it won't come true."

"Honey, I think that's birthday wishes, not what you ask Santa for." Lottie ran a hand down her daughter's back and smiled at the girl. She tried to avoid Cove's eyes, but just as she was about to look away, something caused her to look at him.

When their eyes met, it was as though the stars in the sky collided and everything around her disappeared. There was no sound, no sights, nothing to take her attention from him.

Cove felt the electricity pass between them, and he took in a sharp breath. Was she really looking at him *that* way? Could Alice have been right? In that one moment before they were interrupted, the world tilted and all he knew was Lottie and Quinn. They felt right together, and he was going to do whatever he could to keep this feeling.

"Here comes Santa," Mr. Summers interrupted.

Lottie had never been so happy to see Santa.

Cove wished the jolly ol' elf would walk away and leave them be.

"Santa!" Quinn jumped up off Cove's lap and ran to the town's own Santa Claus. "Mrs. Claus!" Quinn yelled after giving Santa a hug. Then she moved on to the town's favorite grandma.

"Well, if it isn't Miss Quinn," Mrs. Claus cooed and hugged the little girl. "How has your Thanksgiving been so far?"

"Really good. I think Santa is going to give me what I asked for." The little girl looked between her mom and Cove and then back to Mrs. Claus, and she beamed.

Santa leaned down and winked at Quinn. "Shh, let's keep this one wish a secret. Just in case I can't quite make it happen."

"But Santa, I know you can. It's already happening." With Quinn spending so much time with Cove, he was also spending more time with Lottie. The little girl thought that meant she was on her way to getting her wish of a daddy for Christmas.

"It's not Christmas yet." Santa winked and put a finger along the side of his nose.

Quinn's eyes widened, and she saw stars when Santa did that. She just knew Santa was going to make her wish come true. And then next year she was going to have a little baby brother. She clapped her hands and tried very hard to be quiet, but when a squeal came out, she put a hand over her mouth and giggled.

Mrs. Claus knew what Quinn wanted. It was written all over her face. And she thought Lottie might want the same thing. However, when she looked back at Lottie, something inside her told her it wasn't a done deal. Not yet. This year she would have two couples to help get together, and she was looking forward to the challenge.

The entire town had shown up, as well as most of the ranchers and farmers. The room was past full, and Lottie figured she should get going so others could sit down. "Well,

I think it's time we head home." She yawned, and her mother did as well.

"Stop that, you know it's contagious," Sarah Summers scolded her daughter from behind her hand.

Lottie laughed. "Sorry."

"No you're not." Cove yawned and stretched his arms wide.

Quinn chuckled, but did not yawn. "I'm not tired. I want to go play with my friends." She pointed to two other town girls around her age.

"Not now, sweetie. We need to make room for others to sit and eat." Lottie took her daughter's hand and stood up to leave.

"Can I walk you out to your truck?" Cove was ready to make his first move. Lottie had taken a little while to warm up to him, but by the time they were done with their pumpkin pie, she was back to laughing with him and looking him in the eyes.

Now, Lottie turned to look at her mom and then down at Quinn. "Uh, I think we should get moving." Without a response to Cove's request, Lottie left.

Cove sat there, too stunned to say or do anything.

"Well, son. Are you just gonna sit there and watch her walk away?" Mr. Summers hadn't said anything about last night, but he had been watching the couple all evening.

At first, Cove was confused. Then a light went off above his head, and he realized that Michael wanted him to go after Lottie. He wasn't going to waste this chance. "You're right. Have a good night." Cove jumped up and started to clear his plate, but Mrs. Summers shooed him away.

"I'll take care of that. You go and see to my daughter and granddaughter." Sarah smiled at him, and he knew he finally had their blessing—not that he had asked for it yet.

If everything went well with Lottie, he would drive out to the Summers ranch and ask Mr. Summers for his permission to court Lottie. He was going to do this right.

But when he got outside, she was already pulling away in her truck. "How'd they get in and out so fast?" Cove rubbed the back of his neck and shook his head. At least he would see her the next day at church. Maybe he could get her alone after services.

"Cove," a voice called from the parking lot.

When he turned, he couldn't help but smile. Standing not ten feet from him was Brandon and his mom, Melanie. She looked pretty good for having been so sick lately. Cove knew the truth about his friend's mom, but most of the town didn't. "Hey Brandon, Mrs. Beck." He tipped his hat in Melanie's direction.

"Did you have a nice time tonight?" Melanie asked.

"I did. But I didn't see you two inside. Did you go in?" Cove furrowed his brows and thought back, wondering if they had been inside or not.

Brandon laughed. "We were at the table next to yours. But you were a bit too…engrossed in other conversations." He winked at his friend.

"Really? Next to mine? Why didn't you say anything?" Cove rubbed his neck and felt embarrassed for not noticing his friend and Melanie.

Melanie's light laugh belied the tiredness Cove saw in her eyes. "I think Brandon didn't want to interrupt what you had going on with Lottie and Quinn." She winked.

Cove wondered if the entire town knew what he wanted, and was rooting for him. "Well, next time please do interrupt. I'm sorry I missed you inside. Will you be at the gingerbread house competition on Thursday?"

"Of course, I wouldn't miss it for the world." Melanie

loved the gingerbread house-building event. She entered every year.

With the biting cold eating into his every fiber, Cove rubbed his gloved hands together and wished his friends a good night. He headed home in the warmth of his truck and prayed he hadn't messed things up with Lottie that night. Something was bugging her, but he wasn't sure what it was.

When Cove returned to his brother's ranch, he thought back on the night, but couldn't figure out what he had done to upset Lottie. She was having fun, Quinn was having fun, so why did she practically run away from him at the end of the night?

* * *

THE NEXT MORNING when Lottie rose, she realized she had another little monster in her bed. This time there wouldn't be anyone to help watch Quinn in the morning, so she'd have to get her little girl up and take her in to the coffee shop to set things up before church services. Lottie rarely worked on Sundays, but she did on occasion stop in to make sure the store had everything it needed, as well as her employees.

When she and Quinn arrived at the Frenchtown Roasting Company, Quinn pointed out that a few places still needed decorating.

"Why Quinn, I think you're right." Lottie kissed her little girl and thought about what they could do. "Would you like to help me out after church today?"

The little girl bounced on her toes and nodded while grinning from ear to ear.

"I do think you're going to take after me with the decorating." Lottie chuckled and felt joy envelop her as they worked together to get the tables in order for the day.

The baristas working that day also helped to ensure that the pastry case was full and the coffee cups were all stocked. There was a line of customers outside waiting for them to open. It wasn't unusual to have lines in the mornings, especially during the Christmas season. There were some patrons who only came during this time of year for her Christmas-themed drinks and treats. She was going to have to come up with a way to entice them back throughout the year.

An idea hit her, and she looked to her little girl who was straightening up one of the table decorations. "Quinn, what do you think about doing a Christmas in July celebration each year? Bring back the Christmas drinks and treats and a small amount of decorating?"

"I like it, Mommy." The toothy grin that followed sent warmth flowing through Lottie's veins.

"I do, too. When we take down the decorations this year, we'll have to put aside the ones we want to use in July." Lottie was already making mental notes of which drinks and treats to bring back. Certainly, the peppermint mocha and hot cocoa. Although, she'd have to come up with cold versions of them if she wanted to sell them in July.

Once the season was over, she'd look at her records and see which treats sold the best and pick an assortment from them, and maybe even come up with something brand new that would only be available in the summertime. She could do this. It would energize her summer sales, and most likely the town, too. July was a busy month for everyone, but they would probably enjoy a little celebration. Maybe she could even talk Chris and Jessica into creating some sort of summer Santa persona to help out.

The more she thought about her idea, the more the ideas flowed. Typically, July was one of her slowest months. If she could even double her normal July sales, then it would be worth it to do it every year.

Once the store was closed, Lottie and Quinn headed over to the church. The sun was beginning to rise, and it looked to be a nice day. Little wispy clouds filled the lightening sky and gave it a soft look. "What do you say we walk to church today?"

"Yeah!" Quinn pumped her little gloved fists and started to run toward church.

"Quinn! I said walk, not run. There's still a lot of snow on the ground, and I don't want you to slip and fall." Lottie knew her little girl was rambunctious, and spending the past few hours in the shop had to be difficult for her. But she didn't need to spend the rest of the day in the emergency room getting her baby a cast.

The pretty little blonde stopped and waited for her momma to catch up. In a monotone voice, she responded, "Yes, Momma. Sorry."

"Oh, sweetie, you're not in trouble. I just don't want you getting hurt, that's all." Lottie took her little girl's hand and held it as they walked briskly toward the Baptist church in town.

That day they had a guest preacher. Mr. Martinez was a missionary to Chile. Their church supported him and his outreach program that helped young women get back on their feet. Some of them were homeless, and some had come from awful homes. Lottie knew it didn't matter where you lived, people always had trouble. But she also knew that for the most part, America was one of the most blessed nations on Earth. In part because they had always been a Christian nation. As the country moved away from God, more and more evil took root. But they were still better off than most of the world.

Listening to what Mr. Martinez had to say about the women in Santiago, Chile, and how difficult it was to survive if you didn't have the support of your family or a good job, just reinforced how blessed she was to live in Montana. Lottie had been taught from a very young age that you had to have some sort of skill to support yourself. You could not rely on the government to take care of you—you would never be happy if you did that.

Lottie's friend, Chloe Manning, had told her about the homeless situation in Bozeman and how her family back home on the Triple J Ranch had started a ministry for the homeless in Bozeman. The Mannings were really big on giving back.

Her town did a great job of taking care of its own, but other than supporting missionaries through her church, Lottie didn't help anyone outside her hometown. A still small voice told her she might want to expand her horizons. As she sat there looking at the pictures Mr. Martinez shared, and heard his testimony, she knew that she needed to do more to help others. She was truly blessed.

She didn't have to go and sell all her worldly possessions and donate them to the poor, but she could put in extra each month to help the missions team from her church. And Chloe had mentioned something about trying to help the kids going to college. She could come up with ways to help more. Especially if she found more ways to make the store more profitable throughout the year. It was time she turned her focus outward instead of inward. She had a lot to be thankful for. Even with her difficulty, she still had it better than a lot of women in Chile, as well as in Montana.

She had sat toward the back since they'd arrived a couple minutes late. During the service, she noticed that Cove had sat in her regular seat. And there were two empty seats next to him. He must have been saving those for Lottie and Quinn. She smiled and thanked God for such a good friend.

Lottie wasn't sure, but it did seem like Cove wanted to be more than friends with her. He was so sweet to her and Quinn. But she wasn't ready for anything more than friendship, was she? As she and Quinn walked back to the shop, Quinn spoke without needing any response. The little girl loved talking about all the Christmas decorations around town. Plus, as they walked by people, Quinn was Miss Popular and would wave and say hi to anyone who looked her way.

It gave Lottie time to process what she heard in church, as well as what she saw. Cove Hamilton was very giving, and not just with them. She had seen him help others many times. When he was in town, he was always volunteering to help when the town needed it. The last time he was in town she saw him painting the volunteer firehouse when the firemen were working to get the place ready for the fire season.

And she knew he was going to help with the Christmas gift-giving tree event on Monday night. Maybe she should pay more attention to what Cove was up to?

By the time they made it back to her coffee shop, Anise Banning was already inside with a customer. Anise was one of her better baristas who worked part-time, but was always happy to take on extra shifts when she could. She was one of the local girls who never went to college. Instead, she stayed home to help with her family farm. Lottie had wondered if it had anything to do with a lack of funds, or if the girl really only did want to work her family's land.

"Hi Anise. Do you need anything?" Lottie asked as she took her coat off and hung it up with Quinn's on the employees' coat rack.

"Nope, all good here." She handed a large coffee to another customer and took their money.

"Let me know if you need any help. We're going to finish off the decorating," Lottie called over her shoulder.

Anise laughed and went back to helping the line of customers that was forming. Most of them had come from church. Lottie recognized most as regular Sunday afternoon folks.

She used to be closed on Sundays, but she had so many requests to be open before and after church that she said she'd give it a go. As long as her employees didn't skip out on church, she would provide a limited menu and limited hours on Sundays. Well, that and as long as it made financial sense, which it did. She was almost always in the black on Sundays.

It helped that she served up hot sandwiches and soup on Sundays after church, too. Quite a few families would come for lunch. Or single men and women would meet up for lunch. And once a quarter she had a regular catering order for a group of the senior citizens over at the Presbyterian church who had a meeting there. The town had really rallied behind her limited hours on Sundays.

"Can I make the star for the outside tree?" Quinn put her hands together like a prayer and begged her mom for permission.

Every year they made a different tree topper for the small spruce she brought out for the front of the shop. She would pick up a tiny tree and decorate it for either her house or store, and once it was large enough, she would put it out in front of the store, to the side of the door. When her other tree would get too large, she'd transplant it in her back yard, or over at her parents' place. She was building up quite the little tree farm, and she loved it. As did Quinn.

"Of course you can. How do you want to make it this

year?" Lottie usually helped her little girl make a star for the tree topper. They never survived the winter, and on occasion she had to make a new one to replace the one they had made together. She loved these memories she was making with her little girl. She hoped they would always decorate the store together.

"I want to make a star and cover it with tinfoil. Teacher did that this year for our tree at school." The little girl ran to where they kept the industrial-sized aluminum foil and she pulled a very large piece off the roll.

"Okay. Why don't we draw it out on cardboard first and then cover it with the aluminum foil?" Lottie grabbed a box and tore it up so they could make their star. She would either recycle the rest or find other uses for it. Maybe she would create a few stars to use as replacements should something happen to the one they were making that day. Just so Quinn wouldn't worry.

Before they were done, a certain cowboy came through the door of her shop looking for lunch, and butterflies assailed her stomach.

CHAPTER 5

"Quinn? Have you seen my red Christmas sweater? The one with the blinking Rudolph?" Lottie was running late for the town's annual Christmas tree-lighting event. She always had a coffee cart there with hot drinks and pastries. It was her tradition to wear a funny sweater. Some called it ugly, but she loved them. She had a huge selection from over the years. Sadly, the pickings hadn't been very great the past few years. Most of the sweaters were made by machines and lacked a certain flair that she enjoyed. Like the blinking nose on her favorite reindeer.

The pretty little girl walked out of her room wearing a sweater dress over red leggings. The only problem was that her sweater dress was never intended to be a dress.

Lottie stopped in the hallway and smiled. "What did I say about asking to borrow my clothes?" They were nowhere near each other's size, but there were times when Quinn got into Lottie's closet and *borrowed* her clothes. Usually it was on days when they didn't have much to do. Rarely had Quinn ever tried to wear her mother's clothes out to an event.

"I thought I would look better with Rudolph. And it might

help Santa to realize that I'm a really good girl who should have her Christmas wish fil…full…" She furrowed her brow. "Fulfillied?"

"Fulfilled." Lottie put her hands on her hips and shook her head. "Do you think Santa would like it if he knew you took my sweater that I was planning on wearing tonight without permission?"

The little girl put her pointer finger on her chin and tapped it as she stared out into space. Neither said a word while Quinn thought about her actions. When her eyes popped open wide, Lottie knew she'd figured it out. "Oh, Momma! Am I a bad little drummer girl?" Big, fat tears welled up in Quinn's eyes, and Lottie's heart broke.

"No, sweetie, you aren't a bad little drummer girl." She went down on bended knee and hugged her little girl. "You're one of the best girls I know."

"But, I stole your sweater." Between sniffles, the little girl hugged her mom.

"Why don't you take it off, and we'll find one of your sweaters to wear?"

"Do you think Santa's gonna put me on the naughty list now?" Tears ran down the little girl's cheeks as she began to openly cry.

Lottie pulled her little girl in for a tight hug. "Oh no, my little Christmas star. I think Santa knows you're a good girl. I can't see how you'd ever end up on the *naughty list*." She wiped the tears away from Quinn's face and stood back up. "Let's go get you ready for the night. And we can see Santa tonight. He'll tell you you're still on the *nice list*."

She hoped they would be able to get in to see Santa soon. Lottie did not want her daughter thinking she was a bad girl all night long. While yes, she did something wrong, it wasn't nearly enough to warrant Santa putting her on the naughty list. Quinn was one of the best little girls around. And Lottie wasn't being the least bit biased.

Once they were both dressed in their Christmas sweaters, Lottie wearing her blinking Rudolph nose sweater and Quinn wearing a sweater with Santa on his sleigh and giant bag of toys, they left their house with smiles and joy filling their hearts. Tonight was going to be a great night.

The entire town would show up, as usual for a town event, and they would all sing Christmas carols as they watched the mayor light the town's twenty-five-foot-tall Christmas tree. Each year a team went out to the local forest and located a beautiful tree to cut down over Thanksgiving weekend. Then they would bring it into town and volunteers would spend all day Saturday, a half-day on Sunday, and all day Monday decorating it as well as the empty lot surrounding the tree.

Booths would go up in the lot for people to sell their wares. Lottie had a mobile coffee cart that she had brought in earlier and set up. And now she was bringing over the treats she had made earlier that day just for the night. She had just enough power in her little corner of the lot to work a small cappuccino and espresso maker, three coffee pots, a heater for water, and one pot for making hot cocoa. Plus, two microwave ovens to heat the pastries.

Tessa was already at the booth, making up the pots of coffee. Thankfully, it wasn't snowing. There was a tarp covering most of the booths, but even still, if it snowed they would not be very comfortable standing there serving up hot drinks and pastries while the cold white powder drifted down around them. Especially if the wind kicked up. It wouldn't stop most people from attending, either. Everyone in Montana was made from sturdy stock and had learned long ago that if you were afraid of the elements, then you might as well hibernate like the bears up at Glacier National Park.

"Tessa. How goes it?" Lottie parked her cart full of pastries to the back of their space.

"Pretty good. We've already had a few customers, mostly the setup crew." The high schooler looked out at one boy in particular, who was carrying a fold-up picnic table and setting it up close to their booth.

"Mmhm. And might I know these setup crew members?" Lottie winked at Tessa and nudged the girl in the ribs. It seemed this Christmas was full of romance. There must have been something in the last snowstorm that had people noticing those of the opposite sex. She couldn't remember the last time she knew so many budding couples.

Lottie looked out and noticed three new couples walking by, holding gloved hands. And one couple where the lady had her arm wrapped around the man's. If she didn't know any better, she'd think Cupid was in town.

Tessa giggled and lowered her head.

"Momma, can I go make a snowman?" Quinn tugged on her mom's sweater and pointed to a group of kids around her daughter's age on the edge of the lot, playing in the snow.

"Sure thing, just don't go far. I want you to stay within the lot so I can always see you. Alright?" Lottie leaned down and kissed her daughter's cold pink cheek. "And don't forget to keep your hat and gloves on. It's only going to get colder."

"Yes, Momma," Quinn said as she ran toward the other kids.

"I don't know where she gets all that energy." A deep and husky voice chuckled next to her, and Lottie felt a tingle down her spine.

She took an involuntarily shaky breath and turned her

head slowly to look at the handsome cowboy who had snuck up on her. "Cove, what are you doing back here?"

It wasn't that he wasn't welcome, but he never helped behind the counter. Lottie wasn't even sure he knew how to make an espresso or cappuccino. He rarely drank anything more than black coffee or hot cocoa.

* * *

"I THOUGHT I'd help you out tonight." He had other plans, but one thing he was going to do was make sure he got beneath her skin. And from the looks of things, he was starting out on the right foot.

The entire drive in from his brother's ranch that night, he thought of ways to get Lottie's attention. He knew he had Quinn's love, but he wasn't sure about Lottie. And he *needed* her love just as much as Quinn's, if not more.

Just that morning he'd heard the old Baker ranch was up for sale. Mr. Baker had decided to retire and move to Florida. His children already had their own ranches to run, and they did not want his. It was a small spread, perfect for someone like him who only wanted to run a few head of cattle and maybe plant a few vegetables and some hay. Really, only enough to support himself and a small family. He'd probably need one hired hand and that would be it. Of course, there would be a need for more help during certain seasons, but he only needed one person year-round to help out on the ranch. It was a perfect setup for him and Lottie.

Cove felt this was the answer to his prayers. It meant that he was supposed to retire from the rodeo this year and settle down here in Frenchtown, with Lottie and Quinn. And Lord willing, they'd have a few more kids along the way. If not, he'd be more than content with Quinn for his daughter. He had even thought about adopting one day. Or possibly being a foster parent.

What kid wouldn't love living on a ranch surrounded by animals and loving parents?

Even after the cost of buying the ranch, he'd still have a little bit to put in savings for a rainy day. Then, if he considered what Lottie made, they would be very happy. She could keep running her coffee shop and he would run their ranch. Maybe he could even supply her with the eggs she needed, and he might want to think about adding a few dairy cows. They could use all-natural ingredients fresh from their own ranch. That would also cut down on costs for Lottie's shop. He had so many ideas for them. Now, to convince the woman of his dreams that he was the man for her.

Lottie arched a brow. "Do you know how to make coffee?"

He grinned from ear to ear. "Nope, but I do know how to operate a cash register."

"Oh, really?" Lottie crossed her arms over her chest. "What about a Square terminal?"

His smile faltered. "What's that?"

"In the shop I have a regular computer-based cash register. But out here, I have to use something smaller that operates on Wi-Fi." Lottie pointed to an iPad set up on a display next to a cash drawer.

"Oh, I've seen those before. I swipe my credit or debit card and it emails me a receipt." While Cove had used it as a customer, he had never operated one to sell something to anyone before. Could he figure it out? Sure he could. He was an intelligent cowboy who had traveled all over North America and handled different currencies. How difficult could it be? It would tell him how to make change, right? He hoped it would.

Lottie snorted. "Yeah, you've seen these before. But it's not the same as using a cash register."

"If you'll teach me, I'm sure I'll pick it up, no problem." He smirked and winked before taking a closer look at the little iPad.

When Lottie began to point out the parts and how to ring up sales, Cove stood so close behind her that she could feel his breath on her neck. Chills went up and down her spine, and she had to lean on the counter to balance herself. Everything around her began to swim, and she couldn't breathe. "What are you doing?" Her husky voice sounded nothing at all like herself, and she shook her head.

Cove leaned even closer and whispered, "I'm learning."

When a throat cleared, Cove mumbled, "Figgy pudding." Then he stepped back at a respectful distance and smiled at Santa Claus.

"Santa! Santa!" Quinn squealed as she ran into the big man all dressed up as though he were heading out on Christmas Eve to deliver presents to all the good little boys and girls of the world.

"Quinn. Whoa, slow down before you knock someone over." Santa chuckled and patted the little girl on her back.

"Santa, I promise I'm a good girl." Her earnest expression tugged at Santa's heart strings.

"What's this?" the jolly ol' man asked.

"Mark said I'm a naughty girl and going to get coal in my stocking this year." Tears streaked down her cheeks, and she wiped at them as she sniffled.

"And why did Mark say that? Did you do something he thought was naughty?" Santa asked.

Quinn nodded. "I took my momma's Rudolph sweater."

Lottie chuckled and caught Santa's attention. When she

pointed to the flashing nose on her chest, Santa smiled and looked back at Quinn.

"Ho, ho, ho. I see your Momma's wearing my favorite sweater tonight. Is that the one you were talking about?"

The little girl nodded as a giant tear trailed down her cheek.

Santa leaned down to get closer to Quinn.

Cove brought over a chair. "Here, Santa. Please sit on the chair. I don't want you to fall over or get your suit ruined in this muddy snow." All around them, what had been white snow the day before had begun to mix with the mud from hundreds of pairs of boots tracking through the area.

"Why, thank you Cove. That's mighty nice of you." Santa took a seat, then picked up little Quinn and sat her in his lap. "Now, why don't you tell me what's bothering you?"

Quinn began to tell him what she had done earlier at home, and how she was telling Jessica about the sweater and Mark came and pulled her hair, calling her a naughty girl and saying she was only going to get coal for Christmas.

"Hm, I see. Well, he's wrong. But so were you. You do know that taking your momma's sweater without asking is wrong, don't you?" Santa patted Quinn's back in a soothing motion.

Quinn nodded. "But I gave it back to her."

"I see that. And I'm glad you did." Santa pulled on his real white beard as he thought. "You are still on the *nice list*, but just remember to ask your momma next time you want something of hers, alright?"

Quinn's enthusiastic nod made her look like a bobblehead after it had too many sugar cookies. "I promise." She crossed her chest and looked expectantly at Santa. "Does this mean I can still get my Christmas wish?"

When Santa looked up at Cove and noticed how close he

was standing to Lottie, he nodded and whispered in Quinn's ear, "I think you are still on track to get one of your wishes this year. Just remember that the other can't come until next year."

"Oh, I know it. Mark's older brother said I can't get it until after my mommy gets married." She smiled at Cove.

Cove noticed how Quinn and Santa had been looking at him and Lottie and whispering. He nudged Lottie's arm. "What do you think those two are up to?"

Lottie narrowed her eyes. "I don't know. But I do know it can't be any good with the way they're both looking at us and smiling right now."

The gleam in Santa's eyes sent a thrill through Cove. Maybe Quinn's Christmas wish was in line with his?

"I have to go do something really quickly, but I'll be back to help you soon. I promise." He bussed a kiss on her cheek and ran away before seeing Lottie's reaction to his public display of affection.

Cove had called up Mrs. Claus earlier in the day and conspired with her how best to help the families of Frenchtown this Christmas. She had agreed to pull a good selection of ornaments from the giving tree and hold them aside for him, secretly. The last thing Cove wanted was for the Meddling Moms, as he liked to call those gossiping wives, to get wind of what he planned and spread it all over town. It wouldn't have the same impact if everyone knew who was helping Santa.

A woman dressed in a red velvet cape lined with faux fur walked out from the shadows and greeted the generous cowboy. "I got what you wanted."

"Did anyone see?" he whispered as he looked around to make sure no one saw them.

"Please, this is me you're talking to. People always see

me. But"—she held up a red, gloved finger—"No one knows what I'm up to."

Cove chuckled. "Thank you, Mrs. Claus. I really appreciate this."

"How are you going to fill all of those requests without everyone around town figuring it out?" She arched a silver, finely plucked brow.

"I'm only going to buy a few gifts locally. Some I'll buy online through the general store. And the rest I'm going to get over in Missoula and have them giftwrapped at the mall. Hopefully no one will think anything about me buying in small quantities around town." He grinned and kissed Mrs. Claus's cheek. "Again, thank you for your help."

Mrs. Claus blushed and waved a hand in front of her face. "Any time, Cove. Just let me know how I can help."

"Just keep doing what you do. You and Chris help this town out so much more than you'll ever know." Cove sent up a quick prayer to God that their local Santa and Mrs. Claus would have many more years serving their small community.

Everyone knew the true meaning of Christmas. It wasn't all wrapped up in ribbons and bows, it was about the birth of a babe who would eventually suffer and die for this world only to rise again and save them. In just a couple weeks, the entire town would watch as the children of Frenchtown reenacted the nativity scene with live animals. And his little Quinnie would star as Mary. That was one play he could watch over and over again.

Although, the parts of Christmas that were wrapped up in ribbons and bows did go a long way to helping the children and their parents enjoy the season a bit more. Cove looked down at the large stack of paper ornaments in hand. Each one represented a gift that a child in need had asked for, or the parent requested. Some of the requests were for toys, but a lot of them were for warm winter clothes. Things that a child needed in order to survive the cold, harsh Montana winters.

The gifts he would have wrapped up in pretty paper and ribbons might not be gifts directly to God, but they were still indirectly given to Him. The Bible said in Galatians 6:2, "*Bear ye one another's burdens, and so fulfill the law of Christ.*" Cove had always tried to help others out when he could. But this year, he had a strong yearning to help. Something he knew came from God himself.

After he locked the ornaments away in his glovebox, he went back to Lottie's little coffee stand and was happy to see her surprised look when he walked behind the counter to take up his place manning the register. Or the Square? He wasn't sure what it was called, but he was going to show Lottie he could be her helpmate.

After a few tough starts, Cove picked up on how to use the device, and it was really easy. Just different from what he had learned on as a teen who worked part-time in the general store during the Christmas season to help earn enough money to buy presents for his family.

"Cove, you look good behind the counter," Brandon joked as he purchased a hot cocoa and pastry.

"Yuck it up, Brandon." He smiled mischievously at his friend.

When Brandon walked away, Cove called out to Quinn, "See Brandon over there?" He pointed to his friend standing next to Chloe Manning.

"Uh-huh." Quinn nodded.

"Why don't you tell your friends that he's itchin' to be in a snowball fight?" Cove nudged Quinn along when she started to protest. "Don't worry, it won't put you on the naughty list. Brandon loves a good snowball fight."

Lottie overheard their conversation. "But you better make

sure that no one else gets hit." She pointed at her daughter. "Not everyone likes a snowball fight." When Quinn walked away, she turned to Cove. "You sure are ornery tonight."

"Let's just say that I owe Brandon." Cove grinned and watched as Quinn gathered up some of her friends.

"Be right back." Lottie ran to Chloe and tugged her out of the way before anyone could hit her with a packed snowball.

Lottie and Chloe stood to the side and watched as six little kids, all armed with at least a half-dozen snowballs each, threw them at Brandon.

The good-natured cowboy yelped—"Hey!"—then turned to see the grinning kids. His gaze swept over to Cove, and he knew who the real instigator was. "I'll get you back for this, Cove!" He leaned down and picked up a snowball that had missed him but was still in decent shape and threw it softly at the group of kids.

They all squealed and broke away. As Brandon picked up more discarded snowballs and threw them, other kids from the town got in on the action. Parents shooed the kids out of the lot, toward the city park in an effort to keep them from hitting anyone who might not appreciate a snowball in the face, or back.

Before long, all the town's kids had moved their fight to the park, and squeals of delight could be heard by all.

"Well, I think that turned out to be a lot of fun." Mrs. Claus walked up to Lottie, smiling from ear to ear.

"I think so. Care for a coffee or hot cocoa?" Lottie offered.

"Don't mind if I do. A peppermint hot cocoa?" Mrs. Claus loved her peppermint cocoa.

Lottie fixed the drink and put a peppermint stick in after she had topped the drink off with peppermint-flavored whipped cream and crushed up peppermint candy canes.

Mrs. Claus's eyes bulged as she took the heavenly drink. The scent of chocolate and peppermint caused her mouth to water before she took her first sip.

Lottie laughed at the whipped-cream mustache topping Mrs. Claus's upper lip.

"Hmmm, now that's what I call a Christmas treat." Santa's wife licked her upper lip and grinned like a kid. "I'll bet you're selling a ton of these tonight."

"Yes, I think we've probably sold as many of those as we have the peppermint mochas. Two of my best sellers during the Christmas season." Lottie had thought about creating some new flavors, like maybe a gingerbread latte, but so far no one had even asked about other flavors. Maybe she would try something new this Friday in the shop.

It was important to provide the products that her customers wanted, but she also wanted to get more business. Maybe by offering some other flavors, she could get more sales through the rest of the month. And also keep them coming back for more in the new year.

Ever since Thanksgiving, Lottie had seen more and more of Cove. And not just because he was visiting with Quinn, either. Cove had seemed to be looking for her at each event they attended. Sure, he also sought out Quinn. Lottie knew that he took every chance he could to visit with her little girl. The cowboy really did have a bond with her daughter—one that she loved, too.

But his attentions on her lately were confusing. They had never been more than friends. When they were kids, before Sam had asked her out, she had thought that Cove might have liked her, but when Sam—not Cove—asked her to that dance, she realized Cove was just being friendly. As time passed, Lottie saw how Cove smiled at all the girls and flirted his way through high school.

Cove had never seemed like the kind of guy who wanted to settle down with one woman. And she wasn't sure he was ready now. Lottie was not the type to date around, and she certainly wouldn't mess around with Cove if it was just a whim of his. No, she would only consider dating again if the man was serious about her and Quinn. They were a package deal, baggage and all.

So when Cove showed up early on Thursday morning asking how he could help her with the gingerbread contest, she was flummoxed.

Tessa smiled at her boss and looked at Cove, who was up front taking orders. "So, boss. It seems like you have an admirer."

"Oh, garland. Is it that obvious?" Lottie hoped it was just her own overactive imagination, or her lack of dating since her husband had passed away. But if a high school girl noticed the attentions Cove was giving her, maybe he really was flirting?

"Oh, I'd say the entire town knows by now." Tessa giggled and put her forearm over her mouth. They were both in the back, setting out the supplies they would need that night for the annual gingerbread contest.

Lottie provided the premade walls and roofs, along with all the candy and icing anyone could possibly need to make their jolly creations. She was making up the icing while Tessa measured into bowls the various pieces of candy.

"No, please tell me no." Lottie stopped what she was doing and looked out the small window from the back room into the coffee shop. Cove was smiling and joking with various women who had come in to place orders for coffee and pastries. Anise was working out front, helping him. "Oh, drummer boy!"

"I like how you've taken holiday themes and used them in

place of curse words. It kinda makes it all so much more… Christmassy." The teenager giggled.

"Well, we certainly can't say any actual curse words." Lottie grinned. "And I agree, it makes it all so much more whimsical and Christmassy."

They both got back to work on the preparations, but Lottie couldn't get Cove out of her head. The man was gorgeous. There was no doubt about that. With his platinum-blond hair, gray eyes, and being so close to six feet tall… Lottie lost track of what she was doing and had to shake her head to clear it of all thoughts of the handsome cowboy. She needed to focus on her daughter and her work. She had no time for men. Especially men who seemed to attract women like a moth to a flame. If she wasn't careful, she'd be the one getting burned.

Speaking of focusing on work, her phone rang and she answered it. Dread filling her as she listened to her caller.

"I'm so sorry to hear this. Please, stay home and get plenty of rest. Don't come in until you're better." Lottie hung up the phone and looked to her young assistant. "That was Dana. She's sick with the flu and can't come to help tonight."

"Oh, no. What are you going to do? We don't have enough people to help now." Tessa worried her bottom lip.

"Well, we have Cove." Lottie paused. "I know you came in early today, but could you work this evening?" She hated to ask the girl to work overtime, but she wasn't sure what she could do so last minute. Tessa had opened that day, and Anise would close. Dana was supposed to also work the night shift. Her only other help were also out sick that day. The flu had been making the rounds and hit her store hard. She prayed her last two employees wouldn't come down with the flu. Or worse yet, she prayed she wouldn't get it.

"Sure, I can come back and help as long as you need me."

Tessa smiled at her boss. The extra hours would help her with her college fund. "I'd like to work as much as possible around school, and then when we get out next week for Christmas break, I can work every day if you like." She looked at her watch and squeaked. "I'm going to be late for school."

Tessa had received permission to come in late that day, as the extra hours would count toward her work experience class. Since she was helping to prep for a town Christmas event, her guidance counselor had allowed her to miss her classes up to lunch. But she had to be there for her afternoon classes.

"I'm sorry. I should have paid closer attention to the time. If you can come back after school, that would be helpful." Lottie sighed and took a seat. She had been working non-stop for the past five hours and needed a break. And she needed to figure out how she was going to staff her store the rest of the week.

CHAPTER 6

Needing a break, and wanting to check on Cove, Lottie went to the front of the store after Tessa left. “Hey, how ya doing out front, cowboy?”

Cove looked up and smiled when he noticed Lottie had flour on her cheeks. He walked over to her and cupped her face with one hand and used his thumb to clean the white stuff from her face.

“What?” Lottie couldn’t get anything else out. She held her breath as the cowboy caressed her face and stared into her eyes. The man standing directly in front of her not only smelled of leather and horse, but also of cloves. Which made her think of a Christmas candle she had at home. Cove smelled like home.

When he leaned in closer to her, she froze. Was he going to kiss her? Did she want him to? The jingle bell above the door rattled and took her out of her daze. She blinked and backed up a few steps before turning her gaze to the sweet woman who had walked in the door. “Mrs. Claus, it’s good to see you today.”

Jessica looked between Lottie and Cove. She noted the

pink-tinged cheeks and the way Cove was taking in ragged breaths and knew she had interrupted something. Mrs. Claus wondered what they were up to and looked around the store. It was empty. She was the only customer, and the only employee in the store was currently cleaning tables with her back to the couple.

"Sorry to interrupt." Jessica smiled knowingly at Lottie.

"Oh, um. No. You weren't interrupting anything. How can I help you?" Lottie moved away from Cove and toward the cash register.

"I came in to see how things were going for tonight. I can't wait to see all the wonderful gingerbread creations!" Mrs. Claus's excitement for the event was evident in the way she grinned, as well as how she clapped her manicured hands together.

Lottie's face fell. "I wish it were going well, but I've had all my help but two call in sick this week."

"The flu?"

"Yeah, I think so. I need to find at least one good helper for tonight, but preferably two." Lottie wiped the counter down and tried hard to think who might work on such short notice.

With a gleam in her eye, Mrs. Claus cleared her throat. "I have a suggestion or two," she threw out with a c'est-la-vie sort of attitude. Like it was nothing at all.

Lottie jumped at the woman's words. "You do? Who?" If Mrs. Claus was recommending someone, she knew they would be great.

Jessica perused the pastries and asked, "Can I try one of your latest creations?"

"Of course, but who do you think would work well for me? I need to call them and get them in here to train as soon as possible." Excitement bubbled up in her chest, and Lottie hoped she might be able to make the event later that night a true success if she had just a little more help. Without any more help, she'd have to run around like crazy, making sure everyone had what they needed, as well as check in the participants, take their money if they hadn't paid, and sign up anyone if they still had room for more contestants later in the day.

Anise would be working the coffee counter. They always did so much business during these events, she couldn't afford to take Anise away to help with anything. Then there was Tessa, and she'd need to spend most of her time helping Anise so the line wouldn't get too long.

"And how about a peppermint tea? I think that would pair nicely with your new scones." Mrs. Claus smirked.

"You're just messing with me, aren't you? Do you really have someone in mind?" Lottie had never thought of Mrs. Claus as being mischievous, or a liar. But there was something going on, and Lottie needed to pay attention.

"Oh, no. I'm not messing with you. I just wanted to get my treats and have you join me at the table before we discussed these people." Mrs. Claus pulled out her wallet and proceeded to take out a twenty.

After Lottie rang up the order and made change, Mrs. Claus's generosity was put into motion. She put every bit of her change into the tip jar. "You know, I thought I'd see a second jar here, one the town could use to help with the scholarship fund you're trying to set up with Chloe."

Lottie blinked. "That's… I mean…wow. I can't believe we hadn't thought of that. A lot of the town comes through here at least once a week, most more often than that. That's a great idea. I'll have to call up Chloe and let her know." She pulled her phone out of her apron pocket. Since Chloe was at work, she figured she should just send her a text message and ask her to come by at lunch.

"You might want to hold off just a moment, dear." Mrs. Claus sat at the table closest to the counter while waiting for her refreshments.

"Oh, of course. How silly of me. Sorry, I just got so excited." Lottie began to put the order together, and when she served Mrs. Claus with a smile, the elderly lady motioned for her to sit.

"I didn't mean you had to serve me first, what I meant was that Chloe is part of my plan." When Mrs. Claus paused for a sip of her tea, Lottie gave her a confused look.

"What plan?"

"The plan for tonight."

"Oh, yes. Chloe? Help me out? But she doesn't need a job." Lottie's head began to spin with all of this, round and round. Where was Jessica going with this?

Mrs. Claus set her teacup on her plate. "Why don't you ask Chloe and Brandon to help tonight? Maybe you can give them a task they can both do together?" She arched a brow.

Lottie thought about it, and a slow smile spread across her face. "Two hands are better than one."

"I don't know about that," Cove interrupted.

The ladies turned to him.

"I mean, I think they would be a nice help, but I see the machinations going on here." He pointed between the two women. "Do you really think getting in the middle of whatever is developing between them is a good idea?"

Lottie rolled her eyes.

Mrs. Claus smiled sweetly. "Oh, my little Cove." She tisk'd. "I think you don't realize how much help is needed in their case. You do want them to be happy, don't you?"

"Of course I do. But meddling in their affairs doesn't seem right."

"Sometimes"—Mrs. Claus looked between the couple—"a man needs a little nudge in the right direction. And sometimes"—she turned her gaze to Lottie—"it's the woman who needs guidance to see what's right in front of her face."

Neither of them said anything. Mrs. Claus knew she had said just the right thing to get them both thinking about not only Chloe and Brandon, but their own situation.

* * *

EVERYTHING WAS SET for the night's event. Chloe and Brandon had agreed to help, and Cove was going to stay and help out wherever he could when he wasn't building a gingerbread house with Quinn. And Lottie was ready for the town to swarm her little coffee shop. Part of her couldn't wait for the event the start, and part of her couldn't wait for it to end. This was one of the events that created the most work for her, but it also gave her the most joy.

Watching as fathers and daughters, or new couples, worked together to make their gingerbread houses was always so much fun. If she hadn't been in the Christmas mood before that night, there was no way she, or anyone else who attended, would end the night as a grinch.

Christmas joy filled the shop and spilled over in the town. Lottie's coffee shop was the heart of Frenchtown, and she knew it. She was always the first one to decorate and to start playing the Christmas music. Her decorating seemed to be the cue the town needed to start their plans as well. Most of the downtown strip was fully decorated by Thanksgiving. Sure, some had needed a few extra days to put their finishing touches on, just like she did, but Christmas permeated the atmosphere when anyone was on Main Street.

The ranching and farming wives also spoke to her about decorating ideas, and sometimes even asked where she got her supplies. She had noticed that there were small groups of friends who gathered together after Halloween and began making decorations. While she had been invited to join a few, she never had. Maybe next year she would put some time on her calendar to join the women who met in the community center and brought their sewing machines and cricut machines and created such beautiful masterpieces that would also end up in the craft fair.

The jingle bell above the door went off, and Lottie looked up to see who was entering. With a huge smile on her face, she welcomed Quinn and Cove back into the store. He had gone to pick her up from her mother's house.

"Must be nice to have a handsome man helping with your business and Quinn," Anise Banning said from behind her. Lottie could hear the wistful tone of her voice. The young woman had plenty of suitors, she just didn't seem interested in any of them.

"You know, you could have your own handsome cowboy and child if you ever agreed to date anyone." Lottie turned around and winked. "Like maybe Tad Jeffries?"

Anise's eyes widened, and her cheeks instantly reddened.

Lottie had hit the nail on the head. Tad was Anise's neighbor, and the two of them had enjoyed a cup of coffee together a few times, but it never went any further than that. Lottie had wondered. Maybe Tad wasn't interested in his pretty neighbor? Maybe once she got Chloe and Brandon together, she could look to helping Anise and Tad get together? She chuckled and went to greet her daughter with a kiss.

"Momma, guess what?" Quinn gushed when Lottie neared.

"What?"

"Uncle Cove and I are gonna do a gingerbread house!" The little girl squealed with delight and clapped her hands. "Do you think we'll win?"

"I'll bet your house is the prettiest one we see tonight." Lottie tickled her daughter's sides, and they both giggled.

Cove watched the mother and daughter and wished he could join them. A pang of regret stabbed through him. He would have if he'd not been such a chicken when he was a kid. All he had to do was ask her out first.

A hand rested on his shoulder and he turned to see who it was. "Margaret. Good to see you." Cove smiled his bright white smile at the single, and very pretty, cowgirl.

"Cove, it's so good to see you again." Margaret leaned in and hugged the rodeo star. After she pulled back, she batted her lashes and coyly smiled at the cowboy before walking away.

Lottie noticed the two and a scowl crossed her face. "Just another flirt." Her hackles rose and she turned so he couldn't see the frustration that crossed her face.

But Mrs. Claus noticed, and she smiled.

When a cowboy Cove didn't recognize walked into the coffee shop and eyed Lottie and Quinn with more than just a curious gaze, Cove's hackles raised, and he decided he was going to lay claim to the woman he loved. Most of the town seemed to know she was his, but this new interloper must not have gotten the memo.

When Cove went over to the pair, he picked up Quinn and kissed her cheek. Then he put a hand on Lottie's shoulder. It wasn't a kiss or even a hug, but it was enough in public to let that cowboy know these two were taken.

Mrs. Claus sat in the corner of the coffee shop, watching and waiting for her husband to finish his rounds saying hi to everyone. She noticed how Cove moved closer to Lottie when the new cowboy entered. She had not seen how he looked at Lottie, but she had seen the scowl plastered all over Cove's face when he noticed the new man in town.

Jerod Stevens was just over six feet tall, wore black cowboy boots and a black Stetson. His dark-blue button-up shirt underneath his Carhartt jacket made him look the part of a black hat from the old western movies. Jessica wondered if maybe he might be just the catalyst Cove and Lottie needed. Her instincts told her he was a nice guy, but definitely not the cowboy for Lottie and Quinn.

Besides, Quinn had her heart set on Cove. And Jessica agreed that Cove would be the perfect daddy and husband for the Keith girls. But, that didn't mean Lottie had to settle down right this minute. It just had to be in time for Christmas. One date with the mysterious newcomer might help her on her way. And it might force Cove to act a little bit sooner.

Now, to just find a way to work this out.

Turned out Mrs. Claus didn't need to do anything. Cove had already started to lay claim to his girls. But she still needed Lottie to recognize the man for who he truly was. Since she was feeling a bit mischievous, not naughty, she went over to introduce herself to Jerod.

The new cowboy stood tall and held himself with a confidence not many in the area possessed. "Mrs. Claus. I've been wanting to meet you." He put a hand out.

She grasped his hand and smiled warmly. "Mr. Stevens, I've been wanting to meet you as well. Welcome to our little neck of the woods, so to speak." She giggled.

"Thank you, ma'am." He nodded and looked around. "I

just met your husband, Santa. I've never seen a town get into the Christmas spirit as much as Frenchtown."

"Really? Where are you from?"

"Originally? Cody, Wyoming. But the past fifteen years I've been all over the world with the Army."

She could see it. He was a toy soldier. Or maybe a nutcracker? She eyed him and decided with his rigid posture and confidence, he was most definitely a nutcracker. With his military experience, he had gone way past toy soldier.

"Thank you for your service." She smiled at him and decided she liked him. If Cove wasn't the perfect match for Lottie, she would have paired them up. Now, however, she would have to think about who he would complement. "How are you enjoying your new ranch? Did you have to make many improvements?"

He shook his head. "Not really. The McMasters had kept up the place nicely. All I really need is some more furniture and then the stock."

"Oh, you don't have any cattle yet?" Mrs. Claus was surprised he hadn't taken the cattle along with the property.

"I do, but it's a small herd. And I've only got two horses. I'll need more for what I'm going to do with the place. The McMasters sold off a lot of their stock before I offered to buy the place."

"I'd love to hear what you have planned. Care to meet up with Chris and me for lunch tomorrow?"

Jerod winced. "Sorry, I've got plans for tomorrow, but how about next week? This week is all about unpacking and meeting with cattle suppliers."

"Of course. Next week will be wonderful. Have you met everyone here tonight?" Mrs. Claus directed him to where Lottie stood talking to Chloe and Brandon.

Jerod smiled and shook his head.

"Lottie, Chloe, and Brandon"—Mrs. Claus pointed to each one as she named them—"this is Jerod Stevens. He just purchased the McMaster ranch."

"Actually, I've renamed it. It's now called the Crooked Arrow Ranch." Jerod stood tall and stiff like a nutcracker.

Chloe put her hand out first. "Nice to meet you, Jerod. I like the name."

He shook her hand. "Thanks."

Lottie joined in. "It's because of the small creek that weaves its way through your property, right?" She knew the little creek had been nicknamed *Crooked Creek*, and figured he'd used that to help name his ranch. When there was water in it, it zigzagged through his land and helped to water quite a bit of cattle in the springtime.

He told them how he came up with the name, and the four of them chatted while Mrs. Claus walked away. When she looked back, it was only Lottie and Jerod talking. Chloe and Brandon had customers to help. She smiled at her little ploy. Then looked to see Cove scowling again when he noticed the two of them were all cozy and laughing. Her work was done for the night, and she could enjoy the evening's festivities.

Sometimes, a little interference was all a budding couple needed.

Cove watched and waited for his chance to interrupt the nutcracker. He watched Lottie laugh and relax, but he also noticed that Jerod continued to stand tall and stiff, just like a nutcracker would. Was he enjoying Lottie's company? He chuckled a few times, Cove noticed, and the man paid her plenty of attention.

"Uncle Cove?" Quinn grabbed his attention, and he looked down at the angelic little girl he loved with all his heart.

"Yes, my little Quinnie?"

"Are you going to help me or not?" She furrowed her brow and pointed to their gingerbread house they had just started. The two of them were in the children's competition, and he had been shirking his duties of holding the pieces together while the icing hardened.

"Sorry, sweet thing. My bad." He put his hands, and his eyes, back on their project and held the roof in place while Quinn proceeded to decorate the side of the house facing her.

Quinn helped keep his attention off Lottie and the *nutcracker.* They had a fun time building their gingerbread house and decorating it. But they needed the entire hour to finish it. Cove figured they could have actually used a few more minutes, and chided himself for not giving her his full attention for the entire hour. If he had, they might have ended up the winners. As it was, he wasn't sure they would be able to beat the Anderson girls.

Cove moved the gingerbread house to the back wall and set it down on the table for the children's entries. The rules did allow for one adult to assist, but the decorating had to be designed by the children, and they had to do most of the work. Cove had mostly assembled the house and held it in place for Quinn while she made it sparkle.

The Anderson girls had more decorations and set up a gingerbread family in the front yard. But when their father moved the house over to the side, the roof slid off and smashed the family. Both Anderson girls screamed in horror, and their parents took them outside, consoling them the entire time.

"That's so sad. Their house and family was very pretty." Quinn looked on in sadness, and her little heart broke for the girls who would have most likely beat her.

"You know what this means, right?" Cove smiled down on his little Quinnie and put an arm around her shoulder.

Quinn shook her head. "Nope."

"It means you'll most likely win now."

The cute little girl furrowed her brow and looked down at her feet. "But, Uncle Cove. It's not fair if I win just because their house was struck by an earthquake and mine wasn't."

Cove tried to hide his chuckle, he really did. But when the family standing next to them laughed, he joined them. "Oh, Quinnie. You really are sweet." He knelt next to her. "While I do feel bad that their house didn't make it to the side board, part of the requirements stipulate that the house must stand up to being moved to the side."

"What's spit…stipu…late?" Quinn scratched her ear.

"Stipulate. It means specify. Or require." When Cove saw that Quinn was still confused, he tried another tack. "The rules are that the entire gingerbread house, and decorations, must survive the earthquake of moving from the table to the sideboard and still stand when the judges come by."

"Oh, I see. And ours survived the earthquake?" The little girl looked at her gingerbread house and then at the Anderson one.

"Yes, it did." Cove stood up and walked Quinn over to her mother, who no longer had a nutcracker following her around.

One of the judges, the mayor of Frenchtown, cleared his throat. "Can I have your attention, please?" He waved his hands to get everyone to quiet down.

When the room was quiet and he had their attention, he smiled at everyone. "First, I'd like to thank Lottie for hosting the annual gingerbread competition and making the pieces everyone is using tonight to create their masterpieces." He stopped long enough for everyone to agree with him and clap.

"The first competition of the night was for children. And we have a definite winner tonight, folks." The mayor pulled a blue ribbon from the messenger bag slung over his shoulder and looked around. Everyone was quiet and waiting for the results.

Along the back wall were nine gingerbread houses in various stages of development. All of them, besides the Andersons', were still standing. But some didn't have much in the way of decorating. Cove figured those kids must have spent most of their time icing the pieces together. Two of the standing houses did have nice decorations, but they were very minimalistic. Not what one would expect from kids decorating a gingerbread house.

"The judges loved all the entries, and we congratulate everyone who entered. You all did a great job. But one house has embodied the spirit of Christmas in gingerbread form, and stood up to the move from the construction table to the sideboard." Again, the room broke out into applause.

Cove squeezed Quinn's hand, and she squeezed back.

"This year's winner of the Children's Gingerbread House Contest is…" The mayor drew it out and looked at each child left in the room who had entered, and then turned to the table with the creations. He walked in front of them all, and then turned back and slowly walked over and pinned the blue ribbon on the winner. "Quinn Keith!"

"I won?" Quinn put her tiny hands over her mouth and looked up in wonder and surprise to her mom and Cove. "I really won?"

Cove picked her up and swung her around before giving her a giant hug. "Yes, my little girl, you won!"

Lottie came up and joined in on their family hug. The three of them fit perfectly together, and Lottie never even felt awkward. Instead, she beamed at her daughter and turned to Cove. "Thank you so much for helping her win."

"It was all Quinnie. I only acted as the contractor. She

was the decorator and designer." Cove kissed Quinn's cheek and stopped himself from leaning over to kiss Lottie. Everything inside him screamed to kiss the girl. But he couldn't. Not yet.

While the town was busy looking at the children's gingerbread houses, or getting ready for the next competition to begin, Frenchtown's royal couple, Santa and Mrs. Claus, made their way to a quiet corner. "So, my dear. How's our two special cases coming along?"

Mrs. Claus looked around for the two couples in question. "Quite well, my dear. I think things are moving slowly, but forward."

"Does this mean little Quinn will get her first wish this year?" Santa had truly wanted to grant her both wishes this year, but he was only a man. He couldn't create a baby in only a month.

"I do believe she will. And God will take care of next year's wish." Jessica bussed her husband's cheek, and he put an arm around her.

Santa sighed. "Couples sure do need a lot of help getting together."

"Some do. Some don't."

"Did we ever need this sort of intervention when we first met?" Santa didn't think anyone had intervened on their behalf, but after seeing what went into trying to get these two couples together this year, he wondered.

"No, my darling. Times were so much simpler back then. You saw me across the room and came right up to me. As far as I know, you needed no prodding whatsoever." Mrs. Claus looked down and hid her eyes from him. Chris could always tell when she wasn't being completely truthful.

The fact was, even Chris needed a little poke in the ribs to get moving. And everything turned out wonderful for their marriage.

She felt her husband chuckle. "What about that one guy your mother invited over for tea after we met?"

"I don't know what you're talking about." She sniffed and looked back out to see Brandon and Chloe talking in between customers. Just as she planned.

"Well, whatever happened, I couldn't be happier that I asked you to dance, and then to dance with me for the rest of our lives." He took his wife's hand and kissed the back of it.

"Oh, Chris. However we got together, it was God's doing." She beamed at her husband of over forty-five years, and she prayed they would have another forty-five before the good Lord took them home.

Meanwhile, Quinn wasn't sure how she felt about her win. The little girl was ecstatic at first, but when the Anderson family came back in and she saw the tears on little Angie's face, she felt guilty.

"Uncle Cove?" Quinn pulled on his hand as he was talking to Steve Caruthers, the town vet.

He looked down at the sad face of his favorite little girl. "What's wrong, Quinnie?"

"I feel bad."

"Are you sick?" Cove knew the little girl had eaten her fair share of the candy they used to decorate the houses, but he didn't think she'd eaten enough to make her sick. Although, the flu was making the rounds, and he worried she might be coming down with it. He leaned over and picked her up. When he felt her forehead, it didn't feel warm. Her color looked fine. "What's wrong? Is it your tummy?"

She shook her head. "No, it's my heart." Quinn put a hand over her chest, and her little lower lip protruded in the cutest pout ever.

Cove pulled her little lip. “Ah, come on now, Quinnie. Tell Uncle Cove what’s wrong.”

“I’ll catch you later, Cove,” Steve said before he walked away to give the two some privacy.

“Thanks, Steve.” Cove turned his attention back to the little girl in his arms.

“I shouldn’t have won.” Quinn’s pout turned into a determined and fierce glare at the gingerbread house that she felt should have won.

“Are you sure?” Without knowing where this was heading, Cove decided to let her talk it out and see what she was thinking.

Quinn nodded. “Yes, Angie and her sister should have won. If they had an uncle like you helping them, their house wouldn’t have fallen apart and killed their gingerbread family.”

“I see. And what do you want to do about it?”

The little girl squirmed, and Cove let her down. “I want to give her my blue ribbon. Their house was prettier.”

She walked over to her winning house and plucked the ribbon off her roof. Without waiting for Cove, she walked over to the Andersons. “Hi, Angie.”

The little girl who was the same age as Quinn sniffled and rubbed her nose. “Hi, Quinn. I liked your house.”

With a decisive nod, Quinn held out the blue ribbon. “You should have won. Your house was prettier. And you have a nice family.” Her hand stayed there with the ribbon in it.

Angie looked from the ribbon to her mom, and then back at Quinn. “But you won, fair and square. My daddy said so.”

Mr. and Mrs. Anderson smiled down at their youngest daughter with pride as Cove looked on Quinn with pride. This little girl had a heart of gold, and he loved her with everything he had. He couldn't have been more proud if she was his offspring.

"Uncle Cove said so, too. But I think the stipoowate was wrong." Quinn looked to Cove, who nodded his agreement. "You won."

Angie took the ribbon and hugged her little friend. "Thank you, Quinn."

Mrs. Anderson had a tear running down her cheek, and she leaned down to give Quinn a hug. "You are one special little girl, do you know that?"

"That's what my mommy says all the time." Quinn shrugged and waved to her friend as she showed the ribbon to her older sister.

"Quinnie, that was a very nice thing to do for your friend. I'm proud of you." Cove felt tears welling up, and he cleared his throat before anyone could see him get all mushy.

CHAPTER 7

Friday came and went way too quickly for Lottie's taste. She always looked forward to the Christmas movie night, and this year was no exception. Now, it was Saturday and she lay in bed thinking about the night before.

Her friend Chloe was getting closer to Brandon, and it seemed Brandon was very happy to spend a lot of time with Chloe. If those two ended up together, Lottie would be very happy. As would most of the town, from what she had seen. In a small town, everyone was up in your business. And when romance was on the table, the stakes were even higher. Then add on Christmas, and the entire town went into Christmas romance overdrive.

She'd even noticed how people were trying to get her and Cove to spend more time together. Although, she was pretty sure Cove was getting into the mood himself. The way he had looked at her lately, and the amount of time he spent with her, was exhilarating and scary all mixed in one pretty package.

Last night Cove had mentioned again how he was thinking about retiring from the rodeo. She had one hard and fast rule: no more rodeo cowboys. Could she trust that if she opened up to Cove, he would truly retire, and stay retired? She couldn't handle losing another man to a bull. Even now, if something happened it would completely break her, and they weren't even a couple. It would kill her and Quinn if they lost him.

Quinn, how was she going to say good-bye if he went back on the road come January? Her little girl was totally gaga crazy over her Uncle Cove. And speaking about Quinn, Lottie felt the little monster's cold feet up against her thighs again. She was going to have to break the little girl of coming into her room at night if she ever wanted to marry again.

Wait, where did that thought come from? She had promised herself she wouldn't even think about having another husband until *after* Quinn was all grown up. How had Cove gotten so under her skin?

And what about Jerod? He had come into her coffee shop a couple times this past week for coffee, and the smiles he sent her way, while not nearly as intoxicating as Cove's, did stir something inside her. Was she really thinking about dating again? Or was it just the magic of the season and watching her friend fall for Brandon? Would she want to go back to being just friends with Cove when January rolled around and everyone had a case of the winter blahs?

Lottie sighed. No, she was afraid that wouldn't happen. Her feelings had changed over the past few weeks. As she suspected Cove's had. While he had always been there for her, he had never paid her so much attention as he had since coming home.

Last night, when he held her hand during the movie, she almost pulled away. But it felt so *warm*, and so…*right*. There was no way she could have pulled away from him. Had he tried kissing her after the movie when he walked her to her truck, she would have let him. She touched her lips softly, wondering what it would be like to kiss Cove Hamilton, the famous rodeo star known for dating a lot of women.

How many women had he kissed? She had only ever kissed Sam, her husband. Even when they were on the outs in high school she never went out with anyone else. Their first kiss had been in Betty-Sue Peterson's closet when they played seven minutes in heaven. After that, they only had eyes for each other. He told her once after they were married that he'd never kissed anyone but her, and he never wanted to. She had told him the same.

Now here she was, seven years after his death, and she was considering kissing another man. And not just any man, but Sam's best friend. Would he be mad? She knew deep down that he would want her to move on after she mourned him. But with his best friend? Would he see that as being disloyal?

With thoughts of Sam and Cove rolling around her head, she got out of bed and got ready for the day. Saturdays were always busy at the café, and this would be an extra-busy one since it was pancake Saturday. The one day a month where she served up various forms of pancakes. And today's special was a Christmas pancake.

COVE WOKE up ready to go. It was Saturday—pancake Saturday. His favorite day of the month. The previous night, Lottie had told him she was going to have something extra-special on the menu that day, and he couldn't wait to see her and Quinn.

Every morning when he was at his brother's ranch, he tried to get up early enough to help feed the stock. Luckily, his brother hadn't finished feeding them when Cove went outside. He was still trying to adjust to ranch life again, and getting up before the sunrise was tough. Most bodies wanted to naturally wait for the sun before waking. But a rancher, and farmer, didn't have that luxury. The animals didn't work on a sun-based schedule, so neither did the humans.

"Thanks, Cove, for getting up to help. It really does make a difference. Especially in this cold weather." His brother Duke chuckled and walked his brother into the house. "Will you be going for pancake Saturday?"

"Oh, you know it. I wouldn't miss Lottie's pancakes if I could help it." He grinned and warmed his hands in front of the fire that Alice had lit in the family room. "Besides, Lottie said it was going to be a special one today. You and the family should come into town for it."

"That's exactly what I was thinking." Alice, who was already dressed for the day and drinking a cup of coffee, walked into the living room and kissed her husband's cheek.

"Do you really want to bring the boys into town today? For a sugary breakfast? You know how hyper they get after pancakes." Duke took his wife's mug and drank some of her coffee.

"I do know, and there'll be a group of kids playing at the park this afternoon. They're going to build snowmen. I was thinking it would be good for the boys to run off their excess energy after breakfast with some of the other kids. And maybe I can even do a little bit of shopping." She turned to eye her brother-in-law.

"I take it that means you'd like me to watch the boys play while you shop?" Cove chuckled. He didn't have any plans after his late breakfast. Maybe Quinn would want to join him and the boys?

"Would you mind?" Alice asked.

Cove shook his head. "Not at all."

When they all arrived in town, there was a line out the door for service. But when Cove poked his head inside, he noticed that Quinn sat alone at a table in the back.

When she spied him, she jumped up and waved him over. "Uncle Cove, I saved you a seat." She patted the bench seat next to her.

The table was large enough for them all to sit down, but a bit tight when it came to eating.

"Thank you, Quinn. That was mighty nice of you." He wondered how she knew to save a large table, until Lottie came over.

"Thank you so much for saving us a spot." Alice hugged Lottie before sitting down.

"My pleasure. Feel free to call ahead any time you want." Lottie greeted the entire family, and when she looked to Cove she felt her cheeks warm. After the thoughts she'd had about the handsome cowboy that morning, she wasn't sure how to act.

"Well, as a way of saying thank you, how about you and Quinn join us after church tomorrow for Sunday supper?" Alice grinned at Cove.

Cove wondered what his sister was up to. Every time he turned around, it seemed someone in town was trying to get him and Lottie together. He didn't need their help. He'd ask her out all on his own—when he had an idea of where to take her, which he did not. At least, not yet.

It would come. If everyone just stayed out of his business, he'd think of something all on his own. Maybe he'd take her to dinner in Missoula one night this week. Yeah, that's what he would do.

But first, he had to figure out her schedule. It was packed with Christmas activities for the rest of the month. And with the Christmas nativity coming up soon, Quinn had practice most nights. It was his job to take her when Lottie was working late. Hmm, maybe he could enlist the help of Lottie's mom?

Alright, maybe he did need help after all.

When Lottie delivered the table's orders of the special Christmas pancakes, everyone's eyes bulged. They looked like Christmas presents topped with crushed candy canes. The pancakes were tinted red and had chocolate chips in them. Then there was a layer of pink whipped cream; Cove suspected it was peppermint whipped cream. And then a chocolate kiss on top with the crushed peppermints shaped to look like a bow.

He wasn't sure, but he thought he might go into a diabetic coma, and he wasn't anywhere close to being diabetic. "This looks amazing! But I must say, I'm glad you only do this once a year."

Lottie put a hand on her stomach. "Same here. I had some this morning, and while they are very sweet, they're also really good. I bet just looking at these all morning I gain five pounds, easily."

Cove looked her up and down. "I doubt it. You look to be in pretty good shape." He winked.

When the heat hit her face, Lottie knew she was in trouble. He had to stop flirting with her or she'd be in danger of falling for him. And that wasn't in her plans.

But, oh, when he looked at her, really looked at her, it was difficult to stand tall. Her knees would go weak and her heart would pitter-patter like a schoolgirl with her first crush. What was he doing to her? She had to get away from him. "I need to get to the back room and get a few things done, or we'll be behind." Without waiting for a response, she turned and high-tailed it out of there.

Cove watched her walk away before he finished his

breakfast. He felt the connection between them growing stronger every day. If he could just be patient and stay in town, then he knew he would get his chance with her. But, figgy pudding, the last thing he wanted was to be patient. He'd been patient for over twenty-two years. It was time to act.

"Excuse me, I'll be right back." Cove stood up from the table and followed the only woman he'd ever loved to the back room.

When he entered the room, Lottie was in the corner mixing up batter by hand instead of using her industrial Hobart mixer.

Her back was to him, so she didn't know he had entered.

"Stupid man. Doesn't he know what his smiles do to women?" Lottie was mumbling to herself and whisking the dickens out of the batter in her bowl. It was the only way she knew of to work out her frustrations.

"Hey, there." His husky voice traveled the length of the room, and Lottie felt it all the way down to her toes.

She jerked when she heard his voice, and some of the batter sloshed up on her. Thankfully, she had an apron on. But when she took her apron off to change it out, she didn't notice that there was batter on her blouse.

Cove noticed.

When he smiled and pointed to her chest, Lottie looked down and sighed. "Today is not my day. Is there a way to go back to bed and start all over?"

His chuckle sent chills down her spine, and Lottie had to scold herself. She also reminded herself that he was a known playboy. Although she had never seen him with any women, she had heard rumors. "What can I help you with, Cove?"

"Actually, I thought I'd help you." He grinned.

Lottie sighed and stared at him.

"Have you had a chance to get your Christmas shopping done yet?" He knew she hadn't. There was no way she had any time to shop yet. He doubted she'd even started it.

Now she was confused. "What does Christmas shopping have to do with helping me?"

"I'm glad you asked. I thought I'd take you out to Missoula one night next week for dinner and shopping. I'll bet your mom will be happy to watch Quinn." While he hadn't asked Mrs. Summers, Cove knew that Quinn's grammy loved spending time with the little girl. Everyone did.

At first, it looked as though Lottie might say no.

"Come on. You know you wanna go shopping and have a night away from here. And away from the prying eyes of the Meddling Moms." Cove nodded back out toward the front of the store, where he could see Laura Anderson and her kids coming in.

With a sigh and a nod, Lottie agreed. "What night?"

"Would Tuesday work?" That was the only night he knew of where Quinn didn't have practice for the nativity. Practice was earlier that day, so he would be able to take Quinn to practice and then out to her grammy's ranch before coming back to town and picking up Lottie.

Lottie nibbled on her lower lip. "I think that'll be doable. I'll ask my mom if she can come and pick up Quinn from practice."

"Oh, don't worry. I got it." He waved his hand. "I love taking her to practice and watching her run through the role. And I can take her out to your mom's place after." It would be a stretch, and he'd have to be ready to go out when he picked up Quinn for practice, but he didn't mind dressing up for little Quinnie's practice. Cove enjoyed every minute he was able to spend with his special girl.

"Actually, I have a lot of shopping, so it might be good if we left early." Lottie was already running through her head all the things that she would need for her little girl and her family. While she had purchased a couple of smaller items online, she still needed to do the bulk of her shopping. And Missoula had some great stores. Quinn was going through a growth spurt, so she needed a lot of clothes. But she knew she couldn't just get her daughter clothes for Christmas—the little girl would also want toys.

"More time together? I'm down with that." Cove's cheese-eating grin caused Lottie to laugh.

"You look like one of those funny-faced emojis when you smile like that." Lottie pointed to Cove's lips and scrunched her nose.

"Oh, really?" Cove moved closer to Lottie and pulled her into his arms. "What about when I smile like this?" He let his emotions for the woman show through in the way he looked at her, and then at her lips.

At first Lottie stiffened, and then her natural instincts took over and she relaxed in his arms and returned his soft smile. "I think I like this one best." Her words were more of a whisper.

When Lottie's eyes trailed to his lips, Cove shivered and slowly moved in closer. They had been dancing around their emotions for weeks now, and it was driving Cove mad. She never pulled back unless someone interrupted, which they always did. He prayed no one would do so now. Especially when he watched her lick her lips. It was at that moment he knew she would accept his kiss.

Cove tilted his head and leaned in even closer. He was bound and determined to kiss the girl this time. When his lips brushed hers, every nerve in his body lit on fire. His instincts told him to pull her closer and kiss her deeply, but he knew better. He continued to pepper her lips with feather-light kisses. When she leaned in even closer to him and grabbed his shirt front, he pressed his lips closer to hers.

"Lottie…" A cough sounded behind Cove, and he would have to strangle the person who stopped him from kissing Lottie the way he had always wanted to.

Lottie jumped back and screeched. "Anise!"

Flexing his muscles, his shirt tight on his biceps, Cove ran a hand through his hair and mumbled, "Figgy pudding." Cove had never cussed much, but on the rodeo circuit he had heard his fair share of expletives and never picked up on them. But lately, his best friend Brandon had been saying *figgy pudding* a lot. He never understood what caused his friend to use the phrase until that very moment. If he had been a cussing sort of cowboy, he would have used every expletive in the book.

"I'm so sorry." Wide-eyed, Anise looked between the couple and began backing out of the kitchen.

"No, don't be sorry." Cove felt like a grinch in that moment. There he was thinking bad thoughts about the poor barista when all she was doing was her job. It wasn't like Lottie took men to her kitchen and kissed them on a regular basis. Or did she? No, she wouldn't. He shook his head. That was crazy thinking. No, Anise probably had never walked in on Lottie kissing anyone.

"Well, I should probably let you get back to work. I'll see you later." Cove turned tender eyes on Lottie, who looked confused.

"Later?" The coffee shop owner furrowed her brow.

"Yes, I've got Quinn this afternoon, remember?" He stood taller, thinking that maybe his kiss had rattled her enough that she forgot what day it was.

"Oh, yes. Sure. Thank you." Lottie turned to clean up her mess from when Cove had first startled her.

The barista still stood there, quietly looking between the couple.

Cove winked and chuckled before he turned around and sauntered out of the room. Let the barista think what she wanted. He had kissed his girl.

CHAPTER 8

Lottie spent the rest of the day working hard, and doing her Christmas best to keep thoughts of that spectacular kiss out of her head. Her entire body tingled when their lips first met. And then when Cove had continued to pepper light kisses on her lips, she felt as though every single fiber of her being was suddenly alive.

Every time she thought about him, she felt her face warm. Candy canes, who was she fooling? Her entire body warmed at the thought of him. She was in trouble. Was he messing with her, or was he serious about her? Did she even want to find out? Crazy questions and even crazier scenarios slipped through her mind all day long.

It wasn't as though it was a big kiss, but it was the kind that stuck with a girl. The emotion and—dare she say it? —*love* that went into his kisses melted her knees at the oddest times during the day. She wasn't sure if her heart could take another kiss like that from him, or if she would die with a smile on her face.

During one of her silly moments, she was caught by Chloe.

"What's that goofy grin on your face for?" Chloe looked closer at her friend and smiled. "You've got a lot of color in your cheeks. What's going on?"

"Hm? Oh, nothing. What can I get for you today? Peppermint mocha?" Lottie tried to clear her face of the grin she couldn't shake all day, but it didn't work. She felt the smile from ear to ear.

Chloe pointed a finger at Lottie's face. "Something is going on here. If you don't tell me, I'll find out on my own. I'll bet those meddling moms have some gossip to share." She arched an imperious brow.

With hands up in surrender, Lottie looked around. "Alright, fine. Something did happen." She waved for Chloe to follow her, and they went to her office. No way was she going to say one word about what happened earlier out in the open for anyone to hear. She knew Anise would stay quiet about what she saw, but if anyone else got wind, it'd be all over the entire region before anyone could say, *How the Grinch Stole Christmas*.

Once Lottie felt as though they were safe and secure, she broke out into laughter. "You'll never believe what I did today."

"Booked a vacation?" Chloe guessed.

"What?" Lottie's head jerked back. "No. Of course not. I haven't gone Christmas crazy. At least, not yet." She thought her friend might believe she had once she told her what happened.

"Well, then what did you do?" With a small tilt to her head, Chloe watched her friend, and Lottie could see the wheels turning.

"I kissed Cove." Lottie put a hand over her mouth before she could squeal.

"What? No way!" The doubt in Chloe's voice was strong. "Seriously? When?"

Tingles went all up and down Lottie's body just thinking about it again. "This morning. He followed me into the back and, well, he kissed me."

Chloe held up a hand. "Wait, so *he* kissed *you*? Not you kissed him."

Lottie waved a hand in front of her. "Semantics. I did kiss him back."

"Eeek!" Chloe put a hand over her mouth and looked around, then lowered her voice. "How was it?"

With a sigh, Lottie put a hand over her heart. "Like a dream."

"Soooo, does this mean you two are a couple now?"

"I don't rightly know. We do have a date on Tuesday for dinner and Christmas shopping. Does that make us a couple?" Since Lottie had never dated anyone except for her husband Sam, she really didn't know how these things worked.

Chloe tapped a finger on her chin. "Hmm, I'm not very experienced, either, but I do think this means you're a couple now. When will you see him again? You don't have to wait for Tuesday, do you?"

With a sinking feeling, Lottie realized that she would be seeing him every day from now until their date. How would he act? How should she?

"Uh-oh. I saw that change in your face. What's going through that mind of yours?" Chloe put her hands on her hips and pursed her lips.

Lottie sat down. "I just realized that I'm going to be seeing him every day from now until Tuesday. In fact, tomorrow I'll be with him and his family all day long."

Chloe's brows raised. "Really? All day? Did they invite you over for Sunday dinner?"

Lottie nodded. "How do I act? Do I hold his hand? Not touch him?" She threw her hands in the air. "I'm so inexperienced with this stuff."

"Uh…" Chloe scratched her head. "Weren't you married for a while?"

Lottie stared at her friend. "I've never dated anyone other than Sam. And we started at the age of thirteen."

"Ohhh. Wow. Yeah." Realization dawned on Chloe, and she sat down heavily. "I can't imagine what it would be like at our age to have never dated anyone but one person. I'm not a social butterfly, but I have had my fair share of dates and boyfriends."

"Exactly. You know how to act. What am I supposed to do?" She was beginning to get a headache, which she had no time for. "Did I just mess things up for Quinn and Cove? I hope he'll still want to be around her if things blow up for us."

Chloe laughed. "Lottie, you haven't even had a date yet. Don't go blowing up this budding new situation. Just go with the flow. If he holds your hand, let him. If he doesn't, don't worry about it. He's probably just as worried as you are."

"You think?"

Chloe nodded. "Yes, I'd bet a million Christmas stars he is."

After their little talk, Lottie felt better and didn't worry nearly as much when Cove showed up later in the day with Quinn.

"Momma!" Quinn's exuberance knew no bounds. She ran in and hugged her mom before she began telling her all about her day without even taking a breath.

"My, it sounds like you've been busy today." Lottie chuckled and looked from her daughter to Cove.

Cove looked at her just as he had earlier that day when they were alone. The molten lava pools in his eyes excited and worried her. Was it just a passing fancy for him? He'd never looked at her like this before.

"Hi." His breathy greeting sent chills down her spine.

"Hi," she returned just as breathily.

"I'm looking forward to tomorrow. Alice is going to cook up a storm. She's already planning a large roast with all the trimmings." He licked his lips and then looked at her lips.

Lottie took a deep breath and prayed she had the strength to survive whatever was coming.

She hadn't noticed before, but when Cove and Quinn came into the shop they had a lot of snow on their shoulders. Lottie walked to the window. "Cove, how long has it been snowing?"

He chuckled. "All day long. Haven't you noticed?"

Lottie shook her head. "No. I did wonder why it was so slow this afternoon, but I thought everyone must be shopping or wrapping presents or something."

"Nope. They're all hunkering down."

"Will you be able to make it back out to the ranch?" Lottie noticed the wind kicking up and turned worried eyes on Cove.

He walked over to the window and watched as the snow began to dump on the city streets. "Huh, looks like we might have made into town just in time."

"*Oh*, pretty!" Quinn squealed. "Uncle Cove, you're gonna have'ta stay with us, huh."

Just then the power went out in the store.

Cove pulled his cell phone out and turned on the flashlight feature. "Well, it looks like we're going to be hunkering down together. How 'bout I help you clean up and then we head back to your place and see if you have power at home?" He texted his brother to let him know he'd be staying in town until the storm passed. It wasn't that he needed to check in or anything, it was what family did when storms hit. They checked in and let each other know if they were safe. Which he was.

CHAPTER 9

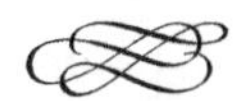

They had barely made it back to Lottie's house. The wind howled and ripped through town, tearing down trees and even a power pole. Which was why the coffee shop lost power. Lottie's house was also without power, but she had a generator—something Cove had set up for her a few Christmases back. She had only used it once, but Cove checked it out every few months and made sure it stayed in working order.

Lottie never thought much about the device, or what it could mean to them. But as she watched Cove going through her house, turning off unnecessary electronics and building a fire for them in the living room, she realized he had always taken great care of her and Quinn. Even before Sam passed away, Cove had been very helpful.

There was a rodeo that Sam had attended, but Cove didn't. Instead, he had come home to help Lottie out when she was pregnant. At the time, she just thought Sam had asked him to check in on her when he was home. Now, she wondered if he came home just to look in on her.

She thought about some of the other things he had done

for her and Quinn, especially these past seven years. Cove had seen much more success since Sam died, but he never ignored her or Quinn. He called at least once a week to check on them. And he sent Quinn gifts in the mail once in a while. And he never came home without at least one present for the little girl.

Had Cove been doing these things out of a sense of duty, or because he cared for them?

"Are you warm enough?" Cove brought over another blanket for the little family who huddled on the sofa, waiting for the fire to warm the room.

She patted the spot on the sofa next to her. "Come and sit down. I'm sure you're just as cold."

He sat directly next to her and put the new blanket over their laps.

Lottie sat in between Quinn and Cove. When Cove settled down, he put his arm around her shoulders and she cuddled up next to him.

"Momma, I like this." Quinn cuddled up next to her mom and stared into the fireplace.

"So do I, sweetie." At first, a sense of contentment filled Lottie. Then dread when she began to worry about the *what ifs*. What if Cove reverted back to his playboy ways? What if he decided after a week or two of being together he wanted to be single again? With everyone pushing them together, was Cove just going after her because of pressure?

No, she told herself. This might all be new to her, but it wasn't new for Cove. He was a worldly, experienced guy. There was no way he would put their friendship in jeopardy for just a whim. *Right?*

Cove sighed and pulled them both closer to him. This was the life. If he could come home to this every night, he would be the luckiest man alive. "This is perfect."

They all sat there in silence as they enjoyed the warmth of each other and looked at the fire. When it started getting low, Cove reluctantly stood up and stoked the fire before putting more wood on.

"Uncle Cove?" Quinn's soft voice sounded as though she might be falling asleep.

"Yes, my little Quinnie?"

"Can you stay with us forever?" The little girl closed her eyes and burrowed deeper into her mother's side.

Lottie looked up at Cove like a deer caught in the headlights.

Cove returned her shocked expression.

They both stayed frozen, staring at one another while Quinn fell asleep as happy as an elf on Christmas Day.

When Lottie's wits returned, she said, "Kids say the darndest things." The nervous giggle gave away how she felt in that moment.

"That they do." Not sure what to do, Cove took his seat and sat just as close to Lottie as before.

She was more than happy to cuddle up with him. When no one said anything else for a while, Lottie started drifting off. Cove wasn't too far behind her.

THE NEXT MORNING when Cove awoke, it was to a cold house and no fire. Although, when he felt Lottie cuddled up next to him, his heart warmed and he smiled. Not wanting to wake anyone, but knowing he needed to get the fire going again, he slowly moved the covers and stood up.

"Hmm? What's that?" Lottie's groggy voice alerted Cove to the fact that he hadn't done a very good job of *not* disturbing her sleep.

"Shhh, go back to sleep. I'm just going to get the fire going again." With a log in one hand and some kindling in the other, Cove got to work and had the fire roaring in no time. He stood there by the fireplace for a few more minutes to ensure that it really was going and wouldn't go out before he retook his place on the couch.

When he turned around to head back to the sofa, he noticed Lottie watching him. "Good morning."

"Good morning. How'd you sleep?" She gave him a warm smile.

Cove took in her mussed-up hair and knew then and there that she was the most beautiful woman he'd ever seen. It didn't matter that her hair was a mess and she had on no makeup; she was perfect.

"Pretty good, all things considered." Lottie looked around and realized they had closed the blinds last night in an effort to keep out some of the cold. None of the lights were on, but that didn't mean anything. It was possible that the power was back, and since they turned everything off they may not realize it yet. "Do you think we have power?"

Cove walked over to the window and peered out. "Nope. The street lights are still off and I don't see any lights on anywhere on the street."

"Care for coffee? With the generator, I can probably whip us up some breakfast and coffee." When a gurgling sound emanated from her stomach, Lottie put a hand over it and blushed.

Cove chuckled lightly, not wanting to wake up Quinn. "That would be great. Do you need any help?"

"I could use some, sure. Just let me get Quinn resituated and then I'll see what we have." She had ensured the generator covered their fridge and a few kitchen outlets, so she knew she could at the very least pull out her griddle and make bacon and eggs. If she made the coffee and then unplugged it to plug in the toaster, she could also get some toast for them.

Some folks had whole-home generators, but since she rarely lost power for long, she didn't need one. Hers only worked on a small amount of outlets at a time. And seeing as how ensuring their food stores stayed fresh was the most important thing, only the plugs near the fridge were covered by the generator. And the hot water heater.

Once Lottie had breakfast made, Cove went in and woke up Quinn, who was already in the process of waking up. "Good morning, Uncle Cove. Is that bacon I smell?"

"It sure is. Are you hungry?" He pulled the blankets off the couch and began folding them.

"I'm starving." The little girl rubbed her tummy and giggled.

"So am I," he whispered conspiratorially.

When they entered the kitchen, the table was set with food and utensils as though nothing was wrong.

The snow continued to dump, but the winds died down during the day so much that Cove feared he'd be able to go home soon. Once the roads were plowed, he'd no longer have a reason to stay at Lottie's house.

The three of them worked together to clear the table and clean the kitchen. Then Lottie brought in some board games that Quinn enjoyed, and they spent the day playing games together. Cove kept the fire going for them all and the living room stayed quite cozy.

"I'm glad it snowed." Quinn beamed at Cove, and she went and sat in his lap. "I want you to stay here always." She leaned her head against his chest.

Cove felt he understood how the Grinch's heart grew two sizes. The love of a little girl was so much more than he ever thought he'd understand. Quinn had always loved him, and they'd always been close. But this time home, something changed. Not only in his relationship with Lottie, but also with Quinn. It was as though something magical, or spiritual, was at work here. Pulling them all together as one instead of three separate people.

Was God answering Cove's prayers?

Lottie watched and felt tears prick the backs of her eyes. If Cove walked away from them, she'd find him and hogtie him to the back of her truck. Fear started to seriously take root until Cove looked up at her with love in his eyes.

She wasn't sure how she knew it—maybe it was how Sam had once looked at her, or it was how her dad looked at her mom? But the way Cove looked at her, she suddenly knew he wasn't planning on leaving them. He was in this for the long haul, and she was going to see where this went.

CHAPTER 10

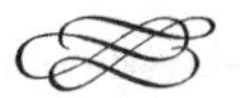

Tuesday came, and Lottie couldn't believe she was finally going on a real date. Cove came and picked her up at three in the afternoon and they headed to Missoula. As they walked out to his truck, he held her hand.

Cove hadn't kissed her again since that time in her shop when Anise walked in on them. There hadn't been a chance. While they were snowed in, Quinn was right there. Lottie didn't want her daughter seeing them kiss. Not yet. She knew it was normal for kids to see their parents kiss, but since Cove wasn't her husband, and she wasn't sure if he was officially her boyfriend, she had made the decision to not kiss in front of her daughter.

"I'm really excited about this. I can't remember the last time I took off work so early and went out." A smile stretched from ear to ear as Lottie sat in the truck.

That feeling of knowing he put that smile on her face shot around his system, and he beamed in response. Out of respect for not only Lottie, but Quinn, he hadn't kissed Lottie again. But he doubted he could wait much longer.

"So, where are we going to start?" Lottie asked.

"Where do you want to start?" Cove started the truck and pulled out of her drive and headed to Missoula.

The plows had done a fantastic job of cleaning the snow off the highway, but some of the roads in town were still a bit sloshy, and Lottie was grateful she didn't have to drive in it.

"Whoa." Lottie put her hand on the dashboard as Cove's truck began to fishtail. "Maybe coming out tonight wasn't the best idea?"

Cove chuckled. "Nah, we're just fine. I'll slow it down a tad and then we can keep going." He reduced his speed down to about twenty miles an hour as he drove through the sloshy streets to the mall. Once he arrived and pulled into the parking lot, he could barely go five miles an hour. Everything was open, but not many trucks were in the parking lot for a Tuesday evening only a couple of weeks before Christmas.

"Ah, I think we might be the only crazy ones out shopping tonight," Lottie joked.

"That only means no lines and more merchandise for us to buy." Cove got a parking spot only four spaces from the front of the mall. "And some of the best parking we'll ever see in December."

"Isn't that the truth." Lottie got out and did her best not to slip and slide as she made her way around the truck. When she was at the tail end, Cove came up to her and put his hand on her elbow to help her walk to the doors.

It only took Lottie two hours to find everything on her list. Cove had been right—no lines at all. There were plenty of clothes and toys for her to choose from. "I think I'll have to come out shopping after a blizzard every year, if it's always like this."

"I might have to join you." Lottie wasn't the only one who'd finished their Christmas shopping that night. All Cove needed now was a special gift for Lottie and he was done.

Not that he bought many gifts, but Quinn and his nephews did seem to get a lot from him each year.

The presents he bought that night, combined with what he already had at home, were enough to fill a Christmas tree. Then add on what his family had purchased, and the tree at the Hamilton ranch was going to be overflowing. Nothing at all like when he was a kid. They got gifts, but it wasn't the same as it was now. For some strange reason in this day and age, if kids didn't get a gazillion gifts for Christmas then they didn't have a good Christmas.

Society had commercialized Christmas so much that the masses had lost sight of what Christmas truly meant. Which was why the nativity play was so important to their town. He prayed that they wouldn't get another blizzard anywhere around the night of the play. The entire town and surrounding areas usually packed the community center where the play would be shown. It would be a wonderful reminder of the *true* meaning of Christmas—Christ's birth.

Sure, the getting and giving of gifts was fun and helped make the season brighter, but he hoped that people would remember why they celebrated December 25th. And why they gave gifts to their friends and family. He might have to rethink how many presents he bought for the kids next year. Maybe he could come up with something to show the kids why giving back was more important than getting.

Cove mulled these thoughts over in his mind as they walked out of the mall, and he noticed more people entering the mall than leaving it.

"Where do you want to eat dinner?" Cove carried the packages out to his truck and put them in the back of the cab.

"Hmm, how about Italian?" In their small town, most of the food served was diner food, or coffee shop food. Lottie didn't get out to dinner too often, and when she did she enjoyed something besides steak.

"I think that sounds wonderful." When Cove started the truck up, there was a line of cars coming into the mall.

"Huh, it seems while we shopped someone came through the parking lot and cleaned up the snow." Lottie pointed out the window to the large piles of freshly plowed snow lining up the back of the parking lot.

"It looks like someone was watching out for us. I doubt if we had come an hour later that we would have gotten everything done so soon." When the signal turned green, Cove pulled out onto the street and headed toward the Italian restaurant.

Once they were seated and had placed their orders, Cove took Lottie's hand from across the table. "Are you glad you said yes to tonight?"

A slow smile spread across Lottie's face. "Yes, I am. Are you glad you asked?"

He squeezed her hand. "You have no idea how happy I am that I *finally* asked you out." Cove chuckled and shook his head. It was like a fantasy, and he wasn't really sure they were actually on a date or if he was home in bed asleep, dreaming this all up.

She furrowed her brows. "Finally?"

With wide eyes, Cove cleared his throat and realized his mistake. "Uh, yeah."

"What does that mean? How long have you wanted to ask me out?" Lottie asked.

Figgy pudding. He mentally berated himself for letting his guard down. Could he tell her he'd been in love with her his entire life and she was the reason he'd never settled down before? Cove didn't think she was ready for the *L* word. Not yet.

"Does it really matter? All that matters is that we're here, together. Right now. I think the timing has worked out well." If she didn't accept that, he'd have to tell her the truth. Cove wouldn't lie to her. He'd seen too many marriages dissolve from stupid lies, and he wanted his relationship with Lottie to start out on a strong footing.

"True. This does seem to be the right timing. Does this mean that you're for sure retiring?" Lottie took a drink of her coffee and set it back down on the table.

A topic he most definitely wanted to discuss. "Yes, if you're ready to see where this is heading, then I'm staying in town and won't go back in January to the rodeo."

"And if I'm not ready?"

He hadn't intended for it to sound like an ultimatum, but when he thought back over what he'd just said, it might have come off that way. "I want to stay in town. And honestly, as much as I love bull riding, my body just isn't what it used to be. I've taken one too many falls this past year, and my doctor recommended retirement."

"But if this doesn't work out"—Lottie motioned between the two of them—"what will you do?"

Cove wanted to say he'd run away and find somewhere else to live if she rejected him, but he was a cowboy. And cowboys didn't run from disappointment, or failure. If she broke things off with him, he'd stay nearby and still look out for her, just as he promised Sam he would. He would continue to be Quinn's uncle and love that little girl for the rest of her life. But he would need some space from Lottie. He'd have to in order to keep from going crazy.

However, he couldn't tell her all that.

"I'd probably find a spread somewhere nearby and still be a part of Quinn's life, as much as you'd let me. And I have my family in Frenchtown as well." Just thinking about her rejecting him hurt. If there was anything he could do to keep her from hurting him, he would do it.

"You wouldn't go back to the rodeo?" Lottie's biggest fear was that Cove wanted to be a part of the rodeo and wouldn't know how to leave it behind.

He shook his head. "No, I'm done with rodeo." He sighed. "I loved it for so long, and wasn't ready to let go. But I came home knowing I had to." Cove looked at Lottie and let his love for her shine through. "I've spent all this time with you and Quinn in hopes that we could move forward, together."

"You know how I feel about rodeo. It took Sam from me, from Quinn…" She eyed Cove. "And even from you. He'd been your best friend for as long as I can remember."

His nostrils flared, and he sucked in a deep breath. "I know." The words came out harsher than he intended, but the loss of Sam was still a sore subject for him. "Sorry. I… It's just…" He ran a hand through his hair. "It's still hard, you know?"

Lottie nodded. "Yeah, I do." She bit the inside of her cheek. "But, I want to make sure that you aren't here with me just so you can be closer to Sam. Or his memory, or something like that." Her hand flailed through the air, demonstrating her frustration.

"Hey, hey." His calm words soothed her. "I'm here for you and Quinn. Of course, I appreciate our shared memories of Sam." He looked down at his hands on the table. "And when I look into Quinn's face and see my best friend..." He blinked rapidly and cleared his throat. "I get choked up at times. But I'd never be with you and Quinn just to be closer to Sam." He reached across the table and took her hands in his again. "I'm here for you."

"If you're sure."

"I am."

"And you're totally done with rodeo? You won't ever go back?" The worry lines across Lottie's face hit Cove right in his heart.

"Yes, I can't ride anymore. It's taken me a while to realize that my body just won't do it again. If I fall one more time, it could be my last."

Lottie put her free hand over her mouth and stifled a sob.

"Hey, hey. I'm here, and I'm not going anywhere." Cove stood up and went to sit on the booth next to Lottie. He put an arm around her shoulder, and they sat there in silence as she got her emotions under control.

When she sat up and wiped her face with her cloth napkin, Cove smiled at her.

"Does this mean that I can go back to my seat?" Cove chuckled.

Lottie laughed. "Yes, get out of here." She pushed him lightly out of the booth.

Right after he sat down in his seat, the waiter delivered their meal.

"Are we good?" Cove asked the moment the waiter left them alone.

"Yes, we are." She took a bite of her lasagna that was stacked a mile high. "Mmm, so is this." She pointed with her fork at her plate.

"Really?" Cove took a piece of her lasagna with his fork and ate it. "Mmm, you're right, it is." Then he took a bit of his chicken parmesan and was grateful that she had wanted Italian. "This was the best choice for dinner."

"Really?" Lottie reached across and stole the bite off his fork that he was about to put in his mouth. "Mmm, yeah. We gotta come back here with Quinn."

A feeling of peace and contentment washed through him

as Cove realized Lottie was planning a future with him. She had never suggested something for their future before, other than maybe him coming by later in the week to spend time with Quinnie. But never had she suggested they take Quinn somewhere together out of town.

He was making real progress with Lottie, and his heart soared.

CHAPTER 11

Cove came by on Friday night to get Lottie and Quinn for the special spaghetti dinner Chloe Manning had organized to help the graduating seniors with college funds.

When Lottie came to the door, she wore a pained expression and wasn't dressed for going out, or receiving company. Her eyes were glossed over and barely open.

She wore Christmas pajamas that had seen better days. The Santa on the front of her warm fleece shirt was missing most of his face. The design had been stitched on, and there were pieces of the applique barely hanging on by a thread. Then there were threads all over the place that looked as though if you pulled them, they would unravel the entire design.

Her fleece pants had holes in them, but her house shoes looked to be rather new. They were red with hard black soles. The kind you could wear outside when you needed to get more wood and not worry about getting your feet wet.

"Lottie, what's wrong?" Cove walked in without being invited and closed the door behind him.

"Migraine," was all that came out of her mouth. Lottie led

them to the living room that was dark except for the fire that needed stoking.

Cove fixed the fire and looked with worry as Lottie climbed back on the couch and covered up. "How can I help?"

"Take Quinn to dinner." Lottie's eyes were closed.

"Uncle Cove?" Quinn whispered. "My momma isn't feeling well."

Cove walked to Quinn and knelt next to her. "I can see. Do you want to go with me for spaghetti dinner? We can let your momma sleep and maybe bring her back some food?"

"Okay, but she don't eat when her head hurts." The little girl rubbed her own forehead and turned worried eyes on her momma.

"Why don't you grab your coat and gloves and we'll leave." When Quinn went into the other room, Cove sat on the edge of the sofa. "Don't worry, I'll take care of Quinn. Do you need anything?"

"No. Just sleep."

Cove leaned over and kissed her forehead. "Okay, get better. And be sure to text me if you need anything at all. I don't want you going without."

A tiny smile crossed her lips, and Lottie sighed. "Thanks."

Lottie's friend, Chloe Manning, was a machine when it came to getting things done. Cove had no clue how she could have managed to organize, and get the entire town to support and attend, a spaghetti dinner to assist the graduating seniors going off to college.

When Cove and Quinn arrived at the community center, it was packed with local families who had not only brought various spaghetti dishes and sides to share, but they all also paid to get in.

"Chloe, this is fantastic. How'd you do it?" Cove looked around at the packed room and realized he was lucky to have found two seats together for him and Quinn.

"I had help. Not only did Brandon help, but so did some of the Meddling Moms, and of course the college students." Chloe laughed. "I explained to them and their parents that if they didn't help me organize it, they wouldn't benefit from it."

"Did you have to threaten them?" While most families weren't big on handouts, Cove had hoped that all the families who needed help with college expenses would have been happy to jump in feet-first and help raise funds for their kids.

"Oh, no. I didn't. Once I told them my idea, they were all in. A few even had ideas of how to get more people to help out. Half of the kids went to Missoula the other day and posted flyers around town, and the other half went to social media and posted the event for anyone to come." The town's medical billing manager smiled and looked around at a lot of new faces.

"Ah, so that explains it." Cove nodded.

"Explains what?" Chloe furrowed her brows.

"Why there are so many people here. I had wondered how you were able to get such a crowd on short notice. And right before Christmas, too." Cove snapped his fingers. "Hey, do you think we can get all these new people to come back for the nativity play next week?"

"What a great idea. We should make an announcement at some point tonight and invite everyone back," Chloe responded. "And how is Lottie? Quinn told me she has a migraine tonight."

"She'll be okay, I think." Cove winced. "She was in a lot of pain when I picked up Quinn. Hopefully being home alone to sleep it off for a few hours will help."

Chloe turned her head when she heard her name being called. She sighed. "I gotta go."

"Thanks, Chloe. And great job with this event. Let me know when you're doing the next one and I'll be happy to help out," Cove offered.

With wide eyes, Chloe turned back to Cove. "Really? You want to help raise funds for the college kids?"

"Of course. I know most of the parents, and even some of the kids who are going off to college. I think it's important to support our youth however we can."

Chloe grinned. "You really do have a heart of gold, don't you?" She waved at the rodeo star and walked away to see what needed her attention.

Once Cove and Quinn got their plates and went back to their table, a man Cove hadn't seen in a while walked over.

"Well, if it isn't Cove Hamilton as I live and breathe." A burly cowboy with a black Stetson smiled down on Cove and his little date.

"Roger Stallings." Cove stood up and held his hand out. "It's good to see you again. What brings you to Frenchtown?"

"I was in Missoula yesterday and saw a notice tacked to the board at the Cattleman's Association." Roger took his hat off and sat at the table next to Cove when the family who had been eating dinner finished and walked away. "I haven't had a spaghetti meal, in oh, I don't know…ages. Plus, I like the idea of helping today's youth get to college."

"Well, that's mighty nice of you. Thank you for helping out," Cove said.

"So, I heard your season ended early. Will you be back on the circuit come January?" Roger asked.

Cove shook his head. "Nah, my career was over when I took that last fall." He looked down at his plate.

"Man, I'm sorry to hear that. I hate seeing good guys leave. What are you going to do?" Roger waved to one of the kids serving and asked for a plate of spaghetti and garlic bread.

Cove winced. He hated that he really didn't have a plan yet. He had an idea, but since the property he wanted wasn't *actually* for sale yet, he really didn't have anything to do for a while. "I'm still figuring it out. My brother runs our family ranch, so until I decide, I'm staying with him and helping out there."

Roger nodded and ate a few bites of his spaghetti. "Say, have you ever thought of raising and training rodeo bulls?"

"Not really." Cove put his fork down and looked at his old friend. He knew Brandon wanted to do that, but he'd never been interested in raising bulls for the rodeo. But, he also thought he'd be on the circuit a few more years. He had thought about training riders, though.

"Why don't you call me in the new year and we can talk about a job with my company? You'd get to keep traveling and be a part of the rodeo, just like you love." The man held out his card for Cove, and he took it and pocketed the business card.

"I'll think about it and call you in the new year." Cove really didn't plan on going back out on the road again, but maybe there was something else he could do. At the very least, he'd enjoy meeting his friend for lunch sometime when the rodeo was in the area.

Before Cove could really say anything about what he was thinking, his phone rang. "Lottie, what's up?"

"Cove? I think I need to go to the clinic." The pained sound of Lottie's voice worried Cove.

He stood up so fast the chair he sat on fell back, and everyone at his table watched him with confusion. "I'll be right there." Cove hung up his phone and apologized to his table. "Come on, Quinn, your momma needs us."

By the time they arrived at Lottie's place, she was laying on the couch with her purse in her hand and shoes on, but she hadn't changed her clothes. "Sorry, I just couldn't."

"No worries, darlin'. No one is going to care about how you're dressed at the clinic." Cove helped Lottie get her jacket on and then proceeded to help her into his truck.

Quinn, the big girl that she was, got herself back into her booster seat in the back cab and did her best to keep her tears at bay. "Momma?" her soft voice asked. "Are you gonna be alright?"

Cove leaned in the back and kissed the top of Quinn's head. "She's gonna be right as rain as soon as the doctor gives her some medicine. Don't worry about her."

The little girl scrunched her nose. "Just as long as she doesn't get a needle, she'll be fine. Mommas don't like needles."

Cove chuckled and thanked God for little girls. "That's right, they don't." He knew Lottie would be getting a needle in her backside, but Quinn didn't need to know that part. He would make sure she stayed outside of her momma's exam room while the doctor and nurse did their thing. No little eight-year-old girl needed to see their momma getting a shot.

Once the nurse had given Lottie the shot of migraine medicine, she led Cove and Quinn inside Lottie's room for a short visit.

"Momma!" Quinn's exuberance was a bit much for a clinic room, and Lottie winced.

"Shhh, remember our inside voices." The grumbling voice coming from Lottie sounded nothing at all like the strong, vibrant sounds Cove was accustomed to hearing from her.

"Sorry, Momma," Quinn apologized, and looked down at her feet.

"Hey, little Quinnie. It's alright. We just have to remember that there might be other people trying to sleep here, that's all." Cove mussed her hair and leaned down for a quick peck on the little girl's cheek.

Quinn smiled and turned to give Cove a kiss on his cheek. She beamed at him.

"How ya feeling, Lottie?" Cove gulped as he awaited her answer.

"Better, but I will need to sleep a lot. Can you keep an eye on Quinn? Or take her out to my mom's place?"

"I'll be happy to watch Quinn, and look out for you as well." Cove had no intentions of leaving the Keith women alone, or taking Quinn to her grandparents' house. No, he was going to care for them both. He'd prove to Lottie that he was up to the challenge of being a daddy as well as a husband.

Well, maybe a boyfriend for now.

* * *

THE NEXT DAY was the town's annual craft fair. It was held at the community center, and Cove couldn't believe that Chloe got the place all cleaned up and everyone had put up their booths so quickly. He had always enjoyed attending the craft fair. His mother used to have her own booth with various crafts she had made throughout the year, like quilts and fancy flower displays. She even used old coffee cans and made up the Claus family and a few elves.

He'd have to ask Alice if she had any of his mother's Christmas decorations. He missed how she would decorate. Cove's sister-in-law did a great job with her decorations, but there was something missing. He couldn't put a finger on it, but when he came home he always expected a certain feeling to envelop him for Christmas.

As he walked Quinn through the room, they stopped at a few displays and looked at various items the town's women had made.

"Uncle Cove, can I get this for my momma?" Quinn held up a potholder and matching kitchen towel with a pretty, snowy scene and a red truck that took center stage. In the back of the truck was a Christmas tree, and on the side of the truck a sign read, *Fresh Christmas Trees.*

A smile tugged at his lips. Just the other day Lottie had bought a little red truck that looked very similar to the one on this towel. She put it under her Christmas tree at home. Cove hadn't really thought about it, but he'd seen a lot of these types of decorations around town lately. Including some ornaments on Lottie's tree at home.

"Yes, I think your momma would love it." Cove paid for the set, and Quinn insisted on carrying the bag around.

Most of the items at the fair were girly stuff. But he did need to get something still for Lottie, so he thought he'd check it out and see if maybe he could find some new Christmas pajamas. Those rags Lottie had on the night before needed to be thrown out. But knowing Lottie the way Cove did, he doubted she'd get rid of them until she had something new to wear in their place.

When he located a pair of red-and-black checked flannel pajamas with a picture of Santa driving the popular little red truck on the front, he knew he'd found the perfect gift for her. He might have to give it to her now and then find something else to put under the tree for Christmas Day. Cove hated the idea of Lottie wearing rags to bed every night.

Quinn pulled on Cove's hand. "Uncle Cove, Uncle Cove,

I want one!" The little girl practically dragged him to a food booth.

When he saw what it was, he laughed and agreed. "I think we should share one." The funnel cake was formed into the shape of a Santa head, a little ball on the end of the hat and all, and covered with powdered sugar.

Mrs. Claus and Santa walked up to the pair as they were finishing off the Christmas treat.

"Oh, I see you two are enjoying today's festivities. How's Lottie doing?" Santa asked when he sat on the picnic table next to Quinn.

"She's sleeping. Or at least, she was when we left this morning." Cove smiled and shook Santa's hand.

"Quinn, was that a Santa funnel cake?" Mrs. Claus asked when she took a seat next to the little girl.

Quinn nodded. "Uh-huh. And it was delish…delist?" She furrowed her brow, trying to figure out the word she wanted to say.

"Delicious?" Mrs. Claus suggested.

"Yup, delicious." Quinn patted her belly after eating the last bite, then she smiled at Cove, and he leaned over and wiped powdered sugar off her chin.

"How are you enjoying the craft fair today?" Cove directed his question to Mrs. Claus.

"I think it's wonderful." Santa's wife clapped her hands and looked around at all the happy people. "This is one of my favorite events of the year. I usually get a few new items to decorate our house with, and always at least one new ornament to commemorate the year."

"Let me guess, you picked out a little red truck with a Christmas tree in the back for your ornament this year." Cove chuckled.

"How'd you guess?" Santa asked.

"Look around. Practically all you can get this year is little red trucks." Cove pointed to a booth close to where they sat that had multiple patterns of aprons with the truck on it, as well as some t-shirts and other items customers seemed to be grabbing up in spades.

"Ho, ho, ho. Don't forget the little gnomes. I love the sign"—Santa pointed to a booth on the other side—"that says, *I'll be Gnome for Christmas*."

"Oh, that's so cute. Uncle Cove, can we get that for Momma, too?" Quinn turned pleading eyes on the cowboy and clasped her hands in front of her as though she were praying.

Cove rubbed the back of his neck. "Uh, I think we have enough for your momma right now." Not only did they have the kitchen set and the pajamas, but Cove had picked up a few ornaments and a lighted painting with the truck. When the lights were turned on, the truck's headlights glowed. Plus, there were Christmas lights that worked on the painting of the tree. He was sure she would love it.

"But I want more." Quinn pouted.

"I think someone has had too much sugar." Mrs. Claus gave Quinn a pointed look, and she quickly sat up straight and erased her pout.

"I'm sorry."

Quinn's lilting voice hit Cove in the heart, and he couldn't help but want to give her everything she wanted. "What do you say we head home and check on your momma? And we can give her some of the gifts we bought her today. It might help to cheer her up." Cove stood and put a hand out for Quinn to take.

Once everyone had said their goodbyes, the cowboy and his little girl left hand in hand. Both carrying several packages and smiling from ear to ear.

CHAPTER 12

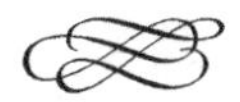

Lottie was feeling much better when Cove came back with Quinn. The two of them animatedly talked about their time at the craft fair, and she wished she could have gone with them.

"Momma." Quinn climbed into her mother's lap. "We got you a gift to help you feel better." She gave the bag with the truck ornaments to her mother.

When Lottie opened it up, she gasped. "This was exactly what I was hoping to find today if I had gone. How'd you know?" She looked to her daughter and then up at Cove.

Cove cleared his throat. "It was an easy guess." He nodded to a few matching decorations.

Lottie chuckled. "Yes, well the truck is the hottest décor this year. It's so cute, isn't it?"

"I heard the Andersons say they were going to paint one of the old junkers they found and put it in the front of their yard. I think Mr. Anderson found an old nineteen-fifty-five Ford truck. It doesn't run. I don't even thing there's an engine inside. But the body is in decent shape. His wife wants him to paint it red, and she wants to put a lit Christmas tree in the bed of the truck." Cove rubbed his chin.

"Oh, that's fantastic! What a great way to decorate that large yard of theirs." Lottie raised a brow. "Do you think we could find one to fit in my front yard? I know it's not very big, but maybe a giant toy version?"

Cove laughed. "Wow, what is this obsession with old red trucks?"

Lottie smiled and thought about all the wonderful decorations she'd seen on Pinterest and was happy with what she had done this year. She even added a wreath to the front door of her coffee shop that featured a pretty red truck in the center. So many of the local women had complimented her on it. In fact, most wanted to know where she'd bought it. When she told them she made it from a pattern she'd seen on social media, they all went out and bought supplies to make their own.

When Monday came, Lottie was feeling one hundred percent back to normal. Having Cove help her with Quinn went a long way to alleviating her stress. She'd forgotten how nice it was to have a man on her team. Someone to help pick up where she'd slacked off, or just plain couldn't do it. Now that Cove was settling in with his brother, she figured he'd be looking for a ranch of his own, or maybe building a house on his brother's ranch. She didn't want to push him, but she did hope he would put down real roots, and soon.

That day, she prepared the peppermint scones and came up with a nice glaze to put over it. That made it easier for people to get a scone on the run and not worry about the cream getting all over the place. The cream topping was very nice, but it wasn't really right for to-go orders. It was best when the person was going to sit down in her café and eat it there.

After experimenting with a few recipes for the glaze, she discovered the perfect one. Now to find someone to test it on.

Chloe usually came in for a morning cup of peppermint mocha, so she'd also give her friend the new scone to try. As she looked around, a familiar blonde head popped into her store. "Chloe, good morning. Chloe?"

The woman in question had bags under her eyes. Oh, she'd done a fairly good job of disguising them with makeup, but Lottie knew her friend better than anyone else in town did. And those were some serious bags hiding out under all that concealer.

Chloe attempted a smile, but it fell flat. "Hey, Lottie. Today's a day for your largest peppermint mocha and whatever new treat you have for me to try." The sad woman walked up to the counter to wait for her drink and treat.

While Chloe waited, Lottie worried. She knew that there was an issue with Brandon. They had spoken about it Sunday after church. But she wasn't sure what, if anything, had happened since the potluck ended. Lottie had to get back to her store to help close up once the potluck was over, and so she wasn't sure if Brandon and Chloe had had a chance to speak or not.

Once she'd made the double-shot peppermint mocha, she added an extra dollop of peppermint whipped cream to the top of the drink and bagged one of her new scones for Chloe. "Here, no charge." She handed the drink and bag to her friend, then motioned for Chloe to follow her to a back table.

"What happened? Did he who shall not be named call?" Lottie looked around to make sure they weren't being eavesdropped on.

"Thank you, this is exactly what I needed." Chloe sighed when she took a drink of the highly-caffeinated drink and tasted the pepperminty goodness of the cream topping.

After Chloe explained her call with Brandon and how she felt selfish about taking him away from his sick mother, Lottie wondered who this person was in front of her.

"You aren't the least bit selfish. Did Brandon tell you that?" Lottie knew her friend to be one of the most generous and giving people she'd ever met. For candy cane's sake, her friend had just about singlehandedly helped a group of graduating teens get most of the money they would need for their room and board expenses for college next year. And if Lottie knew her friend like she thought she did, she knew that Chloe would find a way to raise the rest of the support they needed. It was going to cost about nine thousand dollars per student for one year of housing on campus. That was anything *but* selfish.

"No, of course he didn't." She waved her friend off. "I spent time in prayer with God, and He showed me it was wrong of me to expect Brandon to put me over his mother right now. She needs him more than I do."

Lottie narrowed her eyes. "Are you sure God told you you were being selfish? Or was that your own inner demons telling you that?" She knew her friend could be hard on herself, and this was most likely one of those cases.

Chloe sighed. "I don't know. All I know is that I felt much better when I gave it all over to God last night. And truly, I do feel it was the right thing to do. Brandon and I aren't meant to be together."

"Huh." Lottie put her hands on her hips. "Somehow I think you are meant to be together. Maybe not right now, but you two will eventually get back together, and the next time it will be for good."

"You know"—Chloe pointed a finger at Lottie—"you're one to talk. When are you and Cove going to finally realize you belong together?"

"Uh…" Lottie wasn't sure what to say. She and Cove were getting closer, and the kisses were fantastic, but were they actually *together,* together? Or was it just them getting closer? Until she knew more about what Cove was to her, she was going to stay silent.

"Actually, when are *you* going to realize Cove is perfect for you? I think he's known for a while now." Chloe giggled.

"Aren't you going to be late for work?" Lottie stood up, ready to get to work herself; this conversation had gone way too far south for her liking.

Chloe looked at the clock on the wall. "Oh, figgy pudding. You're right. Thanks for the treats. Catch ya later." She waved as she hurried out the door and down the street to the clinic where she worked.

Right after Chloe left, the cowboy in question walked through her doors.

* * *

TUESDAY NIGHT WAS ALREADY STARTING out great. Quinn was entered into the snowman-building contest with her friend from school, and they were having the time of their lives. Cove was so proud of little Quinnie and the faerie snowgirl she made. Quinn had worn her sparkly wings and brought over an extra set to use for her snowgirl. The rules stated they could use anything in the area, and Quinn had prepared. She dropped her extra wings off next to a few other items, and the moment the contest started, she ran to grab the wings for her snow faerie.

Cove chuckled as he watched her imagination come to

life. If this were a Christmas cartoon, the moment those wings were added Quinn's little snow faerie would have come to life and flitted above everyone's heads. Her friend had picked up a tiara from the trove of accessories, so he supposed it was a faerie snow princess, complete with a plastic wand in her tree-branch hand.

Just before the judge called time, Quinn and her friend put a Disney princess dress-up gown on the snow creature and they both stood back, grinning from ear to ear.

Cove couldn't help but be proud of her. Little drummer boy, was he ever in love with that little girl. Not that he wanted to take Sam's place, he could never do that. But he did want to be Quinn's daddy. His chest puffed out as he looked on and watched the judges smile when they reached Quinn's faerie snow princess. He hoped no matter how it all turned out, that this little snow girl would last until after Christmas right where she was.

"I can't believe how crafty and talented my little baby is with snow." Lottie shook her head and smiled, holding herself back as they finished up the judging for the contest.

"She's going to be an artist one day, isn't she?" Cove asked.

"Hmm. I don't know. If you ask her, she's going to be a cowgirl princess." Lottie laughed.

Cove joined her. And they waited with bated breath as the judges walked past all the entries for a third time. "Do you think she'll win?"

Lottie arched a brow. "This is *my* daughter you're talking about. Of course she's gonna win." She crossed her arms over her chest and scowled at Cove. "Of all the fruitcake ideas." She shook her head.

Cove held his hands up. "Hey now, I didn't mean anything by it. I know her snow faerie princess is the best one out there, but that doesn't mean the judging committee will agree." He looked back as they slowed down when they neared Quinn. "Hey"—he put his hand on Lottie's forearm—"look."

"And the winners of this year's under-eighteen Snow Person Contest is…Quinn Keith and Mallory Sampson." The head judge, who also happened to be the town's sheriff, put a blue ribbon on the belly of their snow princess and handed the girls each a small trophy for winning first place.

Cove saw out of the corner of his eye that the Oogie Boogie green snowman was being awarded second place, but he didn't pay them any more mind when Quinn came running up to him, screaming.

"I won! I won! Look Uncle Cove, I got my first trophy!" She hugged his waist and squealed like a pig.

"I'm so proud of you, my little Quinnie." Cove reached down and picked her up. After he gave her a loud kiss on the cheek, he put her down next to her mom so she could hug her daughter.

"Quinn! You did fantastic. Come on, let's take a picture of you by your faerie snow princess." Lottie took her daughter's hand, and they took lots of pictures before the judges announced the adult competition was about to begin.

Lottie and Cove had signed up as a team, and they headed to their designated spot. The rules were simple: they just had to complete a three-tiered snowperson and add a face of any sort and at least one accessory. One would think that two adults could accomplish that easily in the time allotted. But… not Lottie and Cove.

It probably didn't help matters that they started a snowball fight that escalated out of control. Especially once Brandon and Chloe entered into it. And before they knew it, their snowman was disqualified for not having a head.

"Thanks, Brandon." Cove waved to his friend and pursed his lips. "That was real helpful there."

"I was just returning the favor." Brandon pointed to what was left of the snow…thing?

Cove wasn't sure what Brandon had tried to create, but in no way shape or form did it even resemble a snowman. A grouping of snow tires? Maybe. Cove figured he was doing not only Brandon a favor, but also the judges by ensuring that whatever it was Brandon and Chloe tried to make wasn't qualified.

Lottie shrugged. "At least you never had a shot at placing. We could have placed somewhere if you hadn't beheaded our poor little snowman." She pouted.

Chloe laughed. "Really? You think you would have placed? Where, last?"

"Ha, ha. Very funny. See if I give you any more free Christmas treats." Lottie lobbed a loose snowball at Chloe, but it fell apart and drifted to the ground several feet before it would have touched her.

"I think my waistline will actually thank you for that one." Chloe grinned.

The four of them walked over to where Brandon's mom, Mrs. Beck, was sitting laughing with Mrs. Claus.

"Well, I for one am very glad I came out tonight. You just can't get free entertainment like this anywhere else." Melanie Beck high-fived Mrs. Claus and watched as the two couples continued to joke around.

The next day when Cove took Quinn to her nativity play practice, he texted his friend, Roger Stallings, about meeting up for lunch after the new year. While he'd been busy since Friday night when he and Roger last spoke, Cove had thought about the offer. He wasn't interested in riding anymore, Cove knew that. He had it good in Frenchtown with Lottie and

Quinn. But he wasn't sure he was completely done with the rodeo. He had a few ideas of what he could do, so he wanted to run them past Roger and see if there was anything he could help out with.

When Friday night finally came, Quinn was so excited for her big entrance that she couldn't even eat dinner, which was a first for the rambunctious little girl. "Momma, you'll be there taking pictures of me on my donkey, right?"

"Of course I will, Quinn. You know I wouldn't miss it for the world." Lottie had already told her daughter three times that day alone, not to mention all the other times in the past two days, that she would be there.

"But, you have to run your coffee cart." Quinn pouted.

"Nope, Anise is going to run the cart tonight. I'll be sitting in the audience with your Uncle Cove the entire time. I promise." Lottie crossed her heart and tapped her little girl's nose.

"Okay, I don't want you to miss me. It's going to be so *awesome*!" All Quinn could talk about for the past few days since the first time she got to ride the donkey in practice was how important her role was to the story, and that without her riding in on a donkey, Mary wouldn't have had baby Jesus.

Lottie didn't have the heart to tell the little girl that baby Jesus would have been born with or without the donkey, but she doubted Quinn would have believed her. Now, she'd taken to asking for a donkey for Christmas. In fact, just that morning when Santa came into the shop for his peppermint hot cocoa, Quinn asked him for a donkey for Christmas.

"Hmm, I see." Santa pulled on his white beard. "What about the other things you asked for? Do you want them all? Or are you willing to part with them in order to get the donkey?"

Quinn furrowed her little brows and thought long and

hard. "No, I still want my daddy and a little brother." She smiled and sat on Santa's lap. "But can't I also get a donkey?"

"Ho, ho, ho. I'm sorry to be the one to tell you, but each child only gets one big present per year. And a donkey is a very big gift." He was about to say so is a daddy, but Lottie walked up to their table.

"Is she asking you for a donkey?" Lottie asked.

"I take it she's already asked you?" Santa confirmed.

Lottie nodded. "Yup, and I've told her no." She eyed the jolly old man and hoped he understood the message she was sending him via the Christmas Mental Hotline.

Santa winked up at Lottie. "No worries."

"Be happy!" Quinn said as she jumped down off Santa's lap.

Both adults laughed as Quinn ran to the front of the store, where her friend Mallory Sampson had entered with her mom.

"I don't know where she gets all that energy." Lottie shook her head.

"Well, if you ever figure it out, please bottle it up and sell me some, won't you?" Santa's belly jiggled when he laughed.

"Oh, I'll be bottling it up alright." Lottie massaged her lower back and sniffled before walking back to the kitchen.

Later that day, Cove stopped in to visit. He did get a cup of coffee for an afternoon pick-me-up, but his sole intent was to see Lottie. Once he had his cup of coffee, he motioned for her to follow him to the back corner, where there was some semblance of privacy. "Hey, darlin'." He leaned over to kiss her, but remembered where he was and pulled back.

Lottie, for her part, would have welcomed a public kiss. It would not only have signaled to the entire town that they were a couple, but it would have helped her to know for sure as well. "Hey, cowboy. How goes it?"

"I was hoping you didn't have dinner plans and would like to go out with me tonight?"

Her eyes widened, and she thought about what her evening plans were. The nativity play was tonight, but that would be over in time for a late dinner. "Aren't you planning on attending the nativity play?"

"Of course, I wouldn't miss it for the world. But I was hoping your mom would take Quinn home and you and I could go out for a late dinner?" Cove sounded unsure of himself. He raised his eyebrows in a hopeful manner.

"I… Well…I can call my parents and see if they'd be willing to take Quinn home with them tonight. I'm sure she'd love that. She's always asking for a bigger house and a dog." Lottie chuckled. If she could afford it, she'd get a dog. But they took a lot of time, and that was something the Keith girls didn't really have. Maybe she could appease Quinn with a cat? They really didn't need much, other than to have a clean litter box and food. Lottie could afford that. "Sure, just let me call my mom."

Of course, Mrs. Summers was more than happy to take Quinn for the night. In fact, she offered to take her granddaughter for the weekend. Lottie wasn't sure about that, until her mom reminded her it was the last weekend before Christmas. Even in a small town like theirs the residents would be out shopping like crazy, which meant they'd need a lot of coffee and pastries.

Not to mention all the special orders she had for cinnamon rolls. A lot of families would pick up a pan of them on Christmas Eve to eat for breakfast on Christmas Day. Somehow, her idea the first year she opened had turned into a new tradition for the region. It was one tradition she thoroughly enjoyed. From December twenty-second to the twenty-fourth, she baked half pans and full pans of cinnamon rolls that would all be picked up in time for her to close at four p.m. on Christmas Eve. It was a lot of work. In fact, it was non-stop. She wouldn't sleep much those two nights.

"We're all set. Mom's going to take Quinn tonight." She didn't add the part about taking her for the entire weekend; she didn't want to give Cove any ideas. However, she was grateful to her mom for remembering how hectic this weekend was going to be and offering to help in this way.

"Perfect, how about I pick you both up at three and we can head over to the community center together?" Cove grinned and reached for her hand. He couldn't help but touch her in some way. He only wanted to be close to her, especially now that she was open to his kisses and spending time with him. If only the Meddling Moms weren't such gossips. He hated it whenever he was the center of their meddling. And if he kissed Lottie in public, they'd be married before Christmas. Which would only scare Lottie off. That was the last thing he needed.

With plans set, Cove took off and went to get ready for a special night with his girls.

CHAPTER 13

Lottie's back ached. She knew she was overdoing everything. Every year she told herself she'd hire a student or two to help out part-time. But she never did. While she wasn't a tightwad, she did know that it was Christmas that really helped to line her savings account for the year. She hated to give up any money that could go to help ensure she and Quinn lived comfortably through the year.

But right then and there, she swore next year she was getting more help. The aches and pains, combined with the headache, told her she needed rest. But she couldn't take any time off for the next week. Christmas Day would be hectic, but it would be a day away from the store. She was so grateful that her mother suggested taking Quinn for the weekend. That was one less stress on her. Maybe she could see if one of her part-timers would be interested in working more hours over the next few days, just to help with the baking.

This year, she had at least twenty percent more orders for her cinnamon rolls than she did last year. Word was out, and the good people of Frenchtown wanted in on this new, tasty tradition. Which was great, since she made a decent profit off them. And with the extra profit she could afford to give Anise and the team extra hours.

She and Quinn were barely ready when Cove came to pick them up. She had put up the closed sign on her store a bit later than she had planned; there was a run on coffee that day, and she had to serve everyone before she could close. Anise was taking care of the coffee cart at the play that night, so she didn't have to worry about that. And when the play was over, Anise's father was going to help her get the cart back to the store and clean it up. Everything was set for Lottie to enjoy the night.

If only she wasn't hurting so badly. She took a couple ibuprofens, hoping that would help alleviate some of her aches and pains. And then pasted on a smile when she went to open the door for Cove. "Hey, cowboy." Her less-than-enthusiastic greeting bothered her.

Cove noticed and furrowed his brows. "What's wrong, darlin'?"

"Come in while we grab our coats." She let him in. "I'm not feeling so good. I think I've overdone it again. My body aches, and I've got a headache."

"Please tell me it isn't a migraine." Cove put his hands on her shoulders and massaged them.

Lottie chuckled. "No, thank goodness. Just a regular run-of-the-mill headache." She closed her eyes. "Mmm, that feels good."

They stood there while Quinn put on her coat and brought her little faerie princess roller bag to the front door. "Hi, Uncle Cove. I'm spending the whole weekend with my grammy and poppy." Her eyes widened and she dropped the handle of her bag, which made a thunk on the hardwood floor.

Lottie jumped and put a hand over her heart. "Oh." She

shook her head. "Please don't just drop your suitcase. Now pick it up and make sure it's next to the front door so Uncle Cove can put it in the truck."

Tear began to fill her daughter's eyes. "Sorry, Momma."

"Oh, honey. It's alright. You just scared me." It was more than being scared, but Lottie didn't have time to explain how the act of flinching made her headache worsen, and the sound of the bag dropping to the floor reverberated through her body, causing it to hurt that much more.

Quinn wiped her face and nodded.

"Here, why don't I help you?" Cove gave Lottie a funny look, but leaned down and righted the bag for Quinn.

Lottie began to rub her temples. "I'm sorry if I'm being a grouch, I'm just tired."

"Then tonight is exactly what you need. We can enjoy the show and then go out for a low-key dinner. I'll have you home early." Cove helped Lottie on with her coat and they all left for the play.

Once they were settled in their seats and Quinn was backstage getting ready for the play to start, Cove began texting.

"Who's that? Isn't everyone here tonight?" Lottie looked around and noted just about the entire town was there. Only a few people who didn't buy into the spirit of Christmas were absent.

"I'm just texting a friend from my rodeo days. He wants to get together in the new year." Cove sent another text and put his phone away.

"Oh, he couldn't make it tonight?" Lottie asked, wondering why his friend wanted to get together.

Cove chuckled. "Somehow I doubt Roger would be interested in the nativity. Plus, he only gets a few weeks off during Christmas, so he's with his family right now in Texas."

The lights went down before Lottie could respond. When

the curtain opened, she put all thoughts of Cove's rodeo friend out of her head. The play was going so well, and only one time did one of the sheep get out of line. The little shepherds did a great job penning them in on stage.

Lottie's heart swelled when Quinn was on the donkey. It wasn't very long, but she could see how excited her daughter was to be riding the animal on the stage. It was no wonder she loved her grandparents' ranch so much. The girl had a way with animals. Maybe she'd grow up to be a veterinarian. Lottie had hoped that Quinn would join her at the coffee shop after college, but if her daughter loved animals more than coffee, then she'd support her in whatever she decided.

The entire audience was in raptures watching the children act out the story of Jesus's birth. The only real glitch, which was handled expertly, was when Quinn went to pick up the baby from the manger. She dropped it. The entire community center responded with a gasp.

Lottie knew her little girl was embarrassed and worried. She was just about to jump up and help her daughter when Quinn knelt and picked up the baby.

Cove put his hand on Lottie's arm to keep her in place.

Lottie covered his hand with hers.

Quinn cuddled the baby close as though it were real and not a doll, and continued on with her role as though nothing was wrong. Maybe Quinn would become an actress? It might be a nice activity to put on her college applications. They seemed to like out-of-the-box activities, from what she'd heard.

The tension that the entire audience held was released when Quinn continued on. Everyone sat back comfortably in their chairs. Lottie figured this would be something she and her daughter would laugh about some time down the road. One year, they'd be watching the play and Quinn would come out laughing and say, "You know, I almost killed baby Jesus once." And her entire family would gasp, just like the audience just did. It would probably turn into a yearly story that was told after they all would watch the town's annual nativity production. She just loved that they were constantly making new memories together.

Having Cove here, and enjoying this season together, made it so much more than she had ever thought possible. Just when Lottie needed comforting and restraint, his simple action of touching her arm calmed her and reassured her that all would be alright. She prayed that this man who'd been there for her and Quinn these past seven years would continue to stand by them through thick and thin.

And she thanked God that Cove was done with the rodeo.

When the play was over, the audience went wild. People screamed out "Amen" and "Great job" all over the place. Some of the parents even had flowers for their kids. Lottie could have kicked herself. She forgot.

The local florist had set up a stand in the back and was selling flowers. Cove beat her to it and ran back and picked up the last bunch of red and white carnations.

Melanie Beck looked lost, so Lottie asked her to join Chloe and Cove for refreshments. Lottie was going to have to help her daughter change shortly.

When Quinn joined them, Cove hugged her. "You did so great. We're both so proud of you, little Quinnie." He handed her the bouquet.

Quinn grinned from ear to ear. Then she hugged them both. "Here, hold these. I have to go and change out of my costume."

Once Quinn ran away, Lottie turned to Cove. "Thank you so much for getting those flowers. I can't believe I forgot to get some before the play started." She shook her head. "I've been so forgetful lately, which isn't like me."

"Hey, don't worry. You've got a lot on your plate." He paused a moment. "How can I help this weekend?"

"Do you know how to bake cinnamon rolls?"

"Uh, no. But I can learn, right?" His face brightened until he felt the vibration of his phone. "Hold on, I might need to get this." Cove looked at the caller ID and took two steps away from Lottie. "Roger."

Lottie heard him greet his rodeo friend, but she couldn't hear anything else. A group of parents got between her and Cove. One of the mothers stopped and congratulated Lottie on how well her daughter did, especially her recovery after dropping baby Jesus.

"Thanks." Lottie hoped the town would forget that part, but she doubted it. They tended to remember gaffes much longer than any successes. It was one thing for her family to joke about it down the road, but she didn't want anyone else teasing Quinn over this. It might cause her little girl to stay away from any sort of public events in the future.

"Well"—Lottie turned to Melanie and Chloe—"I better get back there to help Quinn before she rips the dress." She chuckled and turned to walk away. As she did, she noticed Cove was smiling as he spoke to Roger.

When she made it to the back of the stage, where they had set up makeshift changing rooms, Quinn was standing in line waiting her turn. When it was their turn, they worked quickly. Lottie still wasn't feeling too well, but sitting for the past hour did seem to help. Now she was tired and yawning. If it were her choice, she'd head home for a bowl of chicken noodle soup and sleep. She probably just needed more sleep.

As she and Quinn were headed back into the main room, she stopped.

Quinn looked at her mother and then followed Lottie's gaze out to the spectacle in the room. Brandon was kissing Chloe right in front of the entire town. Her eyes widened as big as saucers, and she gasped, happy for her friend. "It's about time."

"I like Brandon and Chloe. Do you think they'll get married and have a baby boy?" Quinn's innocent question hit Lottie hard in the chest.

"I don't know, honey. I hope they do." Lottie wasn't sure what had prompted Quinn to ask her that question, but it most likely had everything to do with all the gossip around town lately. Someone was going to need to do something about those Meddling Moms. Sooner, rather than later.

"I wanted a baby brother, but now that Uncle Cove's leaving again I don't think I'll get one by next Christmas, will I?" She turned sad eyes up to her mother, who frowned.

"Uncle Cove is leaving?" Lottie blinked a few times, her heart pounding. "Wait, you thought he was going to give you a baby brother?" She was so confused by what her daughter had said that she wondered if she heard right.

The little girl nodded. "Yes, I heard Uncle Cove talking about leaving in the new year. He's going to see his rodeo friends." She hugged her mom around the waist. "I don't want him to leave."

The quiet whine of her daughter hit her like an arrow through the heart.

Cove was leaving. Why hadn't he told her? How did she not know? No, her daughter was wrong. Cove had promised Lottie that he was not going back to rodeo. But a niggling feeling in the back of her mind wouldn't stop. Earlier, when Cove had messages from a rodeo friend, he was very vague about it all. Then he stepped away to take a call and was smiling. Something had obviously gone right for him to smile like that. But she couldn't believe it. Or could she?

Cove said many times over the years how rodeo was his life. It was all he ever wanted growing up. And being on the pro circuit, he felt closer to Sam than he had when he was home on his brother's ranch. She knew all of this about him. But she also knew he had hurt himself. Was the good call from the doctor, who might be giving him a release to ride bulls again? She could believe that. The cowboy never appeared to be in bad shape. He seemed as strong as always.

By the time Brandon had Chloe on the donkey and was leading her outside, all eyes were on the one door the donkey could fit through. She decided to leave and go home another route.

On their way out, Cove saw her and joined her. "Hey, slow down. There's no rush to get to dinner."

Lottie turned fiery eyes on Cove. "We're not going to dinner." She turned away and headed outside. Instead of letting her mom take Quinn for the weekend, Lottie had decided she wanted her daughter to be with her.

As she walked out into the parking lot, she realized she had ridden in with Cove and left Quinn's little suitcase in his truck. She'd need that. They could walk home easy enough, but Quinn wouldn't want to spend a night without her bunny. Lottie turned and looked for Cove, who was right behind her.

"What's going on, Lottie?" Cove scrunched his forehead and rubbed his neck. He mentally went over what he had said recently and couldn't figure out what he'd done.

"You lied to me," she accused.

"What are you talking about, darlin'? I've never lied to you." Well, not an outright lie. Cove had only lied by omission. But since she never asked him outright how he felt about her, he didn't think it was a topic he needed to speak about. So really, he hadn't lied at all.

Lottie raised her voice. "Rodeo? Really?"

Her mother ran over and took Quinn by the hand. "Lottie, you should take this somewhere else. People are watching."

Lottie looked around and realized that they did, in fact, have an audience. And it was growing. She sighed. "Fine."

"Where's Quinn's bag?" Mrs. Summers asked.

"In my truck." He clicked the key fob. "I just unlocked it, so go ahead and get it. I'll take Lottie home after we talk."

Lottie's head hurt. She didn't want to talk; she only wanted to go to bed. Her back ached, as did her butt. How in the world did her backside ache when she hardly ever sat?

"Can we do this later? I know you're leaving to meet up with your rodeo buddies in the new year. I'm just…" She waved her hands. "Done." She ran to catch up to her mom. "Can you drive me home?"

Mrs. Summers looked back at Cove, who hung his head. "Sure, honey. Let's go. I bet all you need is a good night's rest and you'll be right as rain come morning. And you and Cove can make up."

Cove watched and sighed as Lottie left. All he wanted was to visit with his friends. He couldn't understand how that was a problem. He might look at the possibility of training new riders, but he wouldn't be riding, so that meant he wouldn't be going back on his promise that he was done. Where was the harm in that? And how did she know, anyway?

When Lottie got home, she was breathing hard and madder than a rat king caught in a trap. Cove had some nerve telling her one thing and then going after something else. The last thing she wanted was to talk to him.

"Here, honey. Let me get you some tea started. I know a

nice cup of hot tea has always helped to settle your nerves." Mrs. Summers went into Lottie's kitchen and turned on the electric kettle.

"Momma, I'm confused." Quinn sat next to her mom on the sofa. "Why are you mad at Uncle Cove?"

The last thing Lottie wanted was to be talking about Cove to Quinn. The way she felt, she wasn't sure if she would say something harsh or not. Cove wasn't a bad man, and she wanted Quinn to keep their relationship. The little girl needed her Uncle Cove. But for the moment, Lottie was too mad to think straight.

"Sweetie, your Uncle Cove promised me he was done with the rodeo. And tonight I learned he isn't. Didn't you say he was going to join the rodeo in January?" Lottie pulled her daughter tight and felt something gurgle in her chest as she took deep breaths.

"But, he still loves us, right?" Quinn's lips scrunched up as she considered what was going on.

"He does. Don't ever doubt that your Uncle Cove loves you."

"What about you? I though he loved you, too." Quinn leaned into her mom's hug.

"Oh, I don't know about that. I think he likes me, but love between two adults takes time." She wondered how she was going to explain this one.

"But, you've spent years together." Quinn thought for a moment. "And how else is Santa going to give me a daddy for Christmas?"

"Wait, what?" Lottie really hoped she was hearing things. "Did you ask Santa for a daddy for Christmas?"

The little girl nodded. "Yup, and a baby brother, too."

Lottie couldn't help it. She broke out into uncontrollable laughs. Her life had become a Christmas movie, and not the sweet Hallmark kind. And there was nothing she could do to change it.

"What's so funny, Momma?"

"Oh"—she kept laughing—"Quinn, you're…too cute." Lottie continued to laugh as tears spilled down her cheeks.

Her mother came in with a cup of tea fixed just the way she liked it. "Here, I think you need to drink it all. And we need to let you get some sleep." Mrs. Summers took Quinn by the hand. "Come on, dear. We should leave your mother to sleep." She looked at her daughter like she had grown a third head before bundling up Quinn and herself for the drive home.

CHAPTER 14

It didn't take Lottie long to finish the tea, eat some crackers, and crawl in bed. She didn't even bother changing her clothes, she just pulled her jeans off and slept in her long underwear and shirt.

When her alarm went off, Lottie moaned and slapped the alarm off. Instead of getting up, she went back to sleep.

Tessa was scheduled to help Lottie with opening the store that day. It was a good thing she had her own set of keys and knew the alarm code, or she would have been on the cold sidewalk for a long time. Instead of waiting, she went inside and got to work prepping the store for the day.

When Lottie didn't show up after three hours, Tessa was worried. She tried calling her boss several times on her cell phone and her landline with no answers. She left a voicemail on Lottie's cell phone all three calls.

The store was busy, and thankfully Anise was scheduled to come in right after they opened. The two of them worked the counters and served the customers. They knew they didn't have any issues with coffee inventory, but they were getting low on pastries. Normally, Lottie came in and began making pastries before the shop even opened. In between busy stints, Anise went to the back to make what she could. Mostly it was the croissants and breakfast sandwiches.

"Thank goodness today isn't pancake Saturday. That's all I can say." Anise shook her head when Chloe entered the store. "Do you know where Lottie is?"

"No. She's not here?" Chloe furrowed her brow, trying to think back to the night before and remember if her friend told her anything about her plans. "Last night, Lottie told me she was planning on working some long days this weekend."

"That's what I thought, too. But she's not answering the phone and hasn't come in yet. I'm starting to get worried. This is her busiest weekend of the year, besides Thanksgiving."

"I'll try calling her while I wait for my drink." Chloe was supposed to be on her way home for Christmas. She had taken the week off and planned on spending most of it with her family. Although, after the previous night with Brandon she had rearranged her plans so that she wouldn't go home until after church on Sunday. Then she would come back the day after Christmas so she could spend more time with her new boyfriend.

When her call went unanswered, she too began to worry. "I'm going to call Cove and see if he knows what's going on."

"Hey, Chloe," Cove answered.

"Hey, Cove. Have you heard from Lottie today? We can't reach her." Chloe bit her lower lip and winced. Without knowing what was going on, there was no way for her to know if Lottie was fine or not.

"She's not in the store?" Cove asked.

"No, and both Tessa and I have called her cell and home. She's not answering." The worry in Chloe's voice spoke volumes to Cove.

"No, I haven't heard from her at all today. We sorta had a fight last night. It was weird. But she did seem like she wasn't feeling well. Do you think she could be having a migraine?" That was the only thing Cove could see keeping her from going into the shop or even answering her phone this time of morning.

"Could be. I'll head over there and let you know what I find out." Chloe hung up with Cove and told the girls running the coffee shop what she was doing. "Be back shortly."

When Chloe showed up at Lottie's house, she wasn't sure what to expect, but seeing that her SUV had stayed in the driveway all night—as evidenced by the small amount of snow that fell last night—worried her. She knocked on the door and received no response. So she tried to open the front door, but it was locked.

Not knowing what to do, Chloe decided to walk around to the back and see if the back door was unlocked. When the knob turned and the door opened, she wasn't sure if she should be glad or upset that her friend didn't lock her back door. But she was grateful she had a way in.

"Lottie!" Chloe yelled out. "Are you here?" She went into the kitchen and then the living room, expecting to see her friend. When she didn't, she turned toward the hall with the bedrooms. "Lottie? It's me, Chloe. I'm coming in if you can hear me."

With a hand on the door of Lottie's bedroom, she turned the knob and pushed the door in. What greeted her caused her to worry for her friend.

In the bed was a woman whose hair was matted. She was

rolling around on the bed, moaning. Chloe pulled her phone out of her back pocket and called Cove.

"Yea, did you find her?"

"I did, and I need your help. Lottie's not doing so well. I think she's really sick. She needs to go to the doctor's office, but I can't get her in my car without some help." Chloe worried her friend might have the superbug that went around last year. She hadn't heard of anyone getting it lately, but one never knew.

"Alright, I'm already on my way in. When you called me earlier, I took off and started driving into town. I'm about thirty minutes out right now." Cove didn't mention that he was also breaking every speeding law out there.

"Good, because she's really sick." Chloe went over and touched her friend's forehead. "She on fire. I don't know what her temp is, but it's most definitely over one hundred. Probably closer to one hundred and two, or three."

"What else is wrong?" Cove had to know what was happening. He wished he would have come to town sooner. Worry wormed its way through his system and he floored it, thankful he had a newer truck with some real get up an' go.

"She's sweating so much that her shirt is wet." Chloe thought to herself that her friend had also smelled better after a long day in the coffee shop than she did right then. But that couldn't be helped. Once the doctor approved it, she'd help her friend bathe and get all cleaned up.

"Do you think it's that bug from last year?" Cove practically whispered his fear.

"No, she's not wheezing. I don't think it's respiratory. I'd bet she's got the flu. You know it's been making its way around town this month. And with all the hours she's put in at the store, she's worn herself down." At least, that's what Chloe hoped. "Uh, Cove? Where's Quinn?" Chloe hadn't heard any sounds, so she didn't think anyone else was in the house. If Quinn was here, then she was most likely sick as well.

"She's supposed to be with her grammy. I'll call them when we hang up just to confirm, and to let Mrs. Summers know that Lottie's sick so she doesn't bring Quinn home."

Chloe rubbed her forehead. "That's a good idea. But just to be safe, I'm going to check her room. The front door's locked, so I'll go unlock it once I'm done and you can just come on in." She walked out of her friend's bedroom and down the hall to Quinn's room.

"I'll hang on until you check Quinnie's room," Cove said.

"Okay." The door was closed, so Chloe reached out a hand, practically holding her breath. When it creaked open, a chill went down her spine. The room was empty and the bed made. "It looks like Quinn's not been here. She's probably with her grammy."

Cove sighed. "Good. I'm gonna hang up and call them now."

"See ya." Chloe hung up her cell phone and put it in her pocket, ensuring that the ringer was up full blast. She didn't need to miss a call from Cove or Lottie's mom. When she left Quinn's room, she went back to check on Lottie.

When Lottie wouldn't wake, Chloe worried for her friend and wondered what she should do. All she could remember was BRATT—bananas, rice, applesauce, toast, and tea. That's what her mom did whenever she had a stomach flu growing up. She doubted Lottie would be able to eat anything at all. However, a cup of tea might be good for her.

Chloe set about making tea for them both. As she worked, she prayed for Lottie. Her friend had gone through a lot since Sam died. She deserved some happiness. Cove could be just what Lottie and Quinn both needed.

Once the tea was ready, she took a travel mug and made Lottie a cup of tea. Then she went into her friend's room and tried to wake her up. No matter what, Lottie needed some water in her system. When Chloe pulled back the sheets, she noticed that they were damp. Lottie had been sweating a lot, for a while. Her fever must have really skyrocketed at one point.

She put a hand on Lottie's forehead and felt her temperature. "I really wish you would wake up and tell me where you keep your thermometer. I know you have one—you're a momma. All moms have basic first aid kits that include a thermometer."

Lottie mumbled something, and Chloe leaned down to hear her friend better. "Cabinet…bath…" was all Chloe could understand. She laid her friend's head back down on the bed and put the travel mug on the bedside table.

Chloe went to the master bath and found the thermometer in the medicine cabinet. Thankfully, it was one of those that you just had to wave over the patient's forehead. And it worked. Lottie's temperature was 102.5, which worried Chloe.

"Come on, my friend. Drink some tea for me. I'm sure it'll feel good going down. Your throat must be parched." Chloe couldn't remember having a fever that high herself, but she could imagine how dry a person's mouth was when they had any fever.

Lottie did manage to get a few sips down before she started to drool.

"Lottie!" Cove's worried voice permeated the house just before the front door slammed.

"Back here," Chloe yelled out.

The cowboy ran, his boots clacking on the wood floor, until he was in the doorway. His eyes were wilder than a horse scared by a snake. His breathing was labored, and he started forward. "Lottie?" He dropped to his knees next to her bed.

"I got her to drink some tea, but if you can help me get her up and dressed in at least some pants, then we can take her to the clinic." Chloe bit her lip and wondered if she shouldn't have worked to get Lottie into some sweats before Cove arrived. She had on long underwear, but Chloe doubted her friend would want anyone to see her like that. Especially Cove.

"Yes, of course. Whatever you need." Cove worked next to Chloe in silence as they helped a sleeping Lottie get into sweats and then a jacket. Although, Cove wasn't sure they should be putting such warm clothes on someone who obviously had such a high fever. He almost voiced his concern when he noticed Lottie begin to shiver.

Cove carried the love of his life out to his truck and gave his keys to Chloe. "Here, you drive and I'll hold her in the back seat."

Chloe pulled up to the front of the clinic to let Cove out as close to the main entrance as possible.

The moment the truck stopped, Cove jumped out of the back seat with Lottie in his arms and practically ran inside.

"I'll just go park your truck and come inside," Chloe muttered to an empty walkway. Cove was inside, and the automatic door shut before she got a word out.

Worry ate at her until she was back inside with Cove. "Here's your keys. The truck's visible from the front door."

"Thanks." Cove took the keys from Chloe.

"Has anyone said anything yet?" She seriously doubted there was anything to tell yet, but one never knew.

Cove shook his head. "No, the nurse put her on a gurney

the moment I walked through the door and told me to sit down."

"So, it's a wait-and-see game now?" Chloe hated this part. There wasn't anything to do, nowhere to go, and they couldn't go back into the room with Lottie since they weren't family and Lottie was unconscious and couldn't give her approval. So they sat there drinking lukewarm coffee out of an old-fashioned vending machine. "Ugh, Lottie needs to outfit them with some of her coffee."

Cove scrunch his nose and smacked his tongue. "Yeah, and they need to turn up the temperature on their drinks. This is practically cold."

Neither were sure how long they waited, but finally a doctor came through to them. One they knew.

"Doc Brown. How is she?" Cove stood up and went right up to the doctor.

The doctor still had on his face mask and looked scary in all that PPE. "It's a good thing you found her when you did. She's got a very bad case of the flu, but thankfully nothing worse."

Chloe sighed.

Cove let out a breath he didn't realize he'd been holding and reached out to shake the doctor's hand. "Thank you. When can I see her?"

"I'm afraid she's not up for visitors today. Why don't you come back tomorrow afternoon?" Doctor Brown looked between the two waiting impatiently to see Lottie.

"Is she that bad?" Chloe asked.

"It's more that she's in need of rest. I've got her on an IV drip of fluids, and we gave her a shot to help with her flu symptoms, so she sleeping right now. I'd like to let her body do its job for the next twenty-four hours, which is a very critical time." The doctor frowned. "Have either of you had your flu shots this year?"

Both shook their heads.

"I actually never get one." Chloe shrugged. Even though she worked in the healthcare industry she never saw patients, and since she rarely got sick she didn't think she needed it.

Cove ran a hand through his messy hair for the umpteenth time. "I don't, either. I've not been sick since I was a kid."

The doctor nodded. "Well, you're both relatively young and healthy. But you might want to consider it. How about Quinn? She's young and very susceptible to the flu, as are Lottie's parents."

Cove looked to Chloe, who shrugged. "I'll call Mrs. Summers on my way home and tell her what's going on."

"Alright but let her know that I don't want any of them coming in to see Lottie unless they've had the flu vaccination this year. You two should be fine, if you're sure you don't want it?"

They both nodded.

The doctor nodded. "Alright, I'll leave orders for the nurses to let you visit for a very limited time tomorrow afternoon. But if you're the least bit sick, I want you to see your doctor." He waggled a finger at them both. "Got it?"

"Got it," Chloe agreed.

"Yup," Cove responded.

"Good, now go home and get some rest. I'll see you tomorrow." The doctor went back toward the nurses' station, leaving Chloe and Cove staring at each other.

"The shop!" they both yelled at the same time.

"Take me back to get my car, and I'll go over there and let them know what's going on." Chloe would be able to help for a little while, but not for very long. She also knew that the cinnamon rolls needed to be baked up this weekend. There was no way Lottie was going to be able to get any of it done.

"I'll meet you back at the shop after I drop you off at your car. While I'm not a baker, I've spent enough time helping out the past few weeks that I could run the front while the other girls bake the pastries." He told himself he was a strong cowboy, and nothing would get in his way of helping Lottie.

The way she reacted to him last night must have been because she was sick. She didn't mean anything she said. They weren't *done*, as she had said last night—that was the fever talking. Now it was all making sense. And he would do whatever it took to help Lottie out.

When Cove dropped Chloe off at Lottie's, she turned to him before closing the truck door. "I'm going to go inside and make sure we locked everything up and that I didn't leave the teapot boiling or anything crazy like that."

Cove nodded.

"I'll see you at the coffee shop." She closed the door without waiting for a response and walked inside Lottie's house. They hadn't thought to lock up anything.

As Chloe walked around ensuring everything was locked and cleaned, she decided to change her friend's sweat-drenched sheets. She knew Lottie wouldn't feel like changing them out when she got home.

After she cleaned up a little, she found Lottie's purse and looked for her friend's insurance card. She knew from experience that the clinic would need this information. And better she get it than anyone else rummaging through her personally identifiable information. Chloe did, after all, have access to Lottie's information already for her job. And she doubted Cove would want to look through any woman's purse, even Lottie's.

Chloe knew from experience with her dad and five

brothers that cowboys feared a woman's purse. Probably for good reason. She'd seen plenty of teen girls hitting boys with their purses, and the boys complaining that it felt like there was a bunch of rocks in the purse. She chuckled for the first time as she thought back to her own brothers and the fear that crossed their faces one summer when she and Elizabeth caught them snooping.

Their dad worked them extra hard, after both Chloe and Elizabeth hit all five boys with their fists. Then their mom sat them down and had a talkin' to with them. They went out of their way to avoid her purse after that. She had always wondered what her mom said to the boys. "Hmm, maybe I'll have to ask when I go home." She hadn't thought about that issue for years.

By the time Chloe got to the coffee shop, Cove had helped to take care of the line of people that had been out the door wanting coffee and the last of the pastries in the entire shop.

"Thank goodness you're here. I could use some help cleaning up." Cove gave Chloe a weary look.

"You've only been here, what? An hour?" Chloe chuckled. She hadn't taken that much time to straighten up, so she knew he couldn't have been too busy.

"When I got here, the line snaked around outside. I just fixed up the last pastry. Dana is all alone in the kitchen making more. The two who opened had to leave, but they'll be back to open again tomorrow, and other than church they'll be baking all day long. Dana said she could help, too." Cove went to get the cleaning products and came out to clean off the dirty tables.

"I can help clean up out front, and then I'll go and help Dana. Maybe Brandon can come help you man the front?" Chloe was supposed to go out with Brandon that night, but

Lottie needed their help more than they needed a date. Maybe even Melanie would want to come and help bake the night away.

"Can you call him? That would be great." When Cove's shoulders sagged, Chloe knew he was really in over his head.

With her call to Brandon settled, Chloe went to the back to help Dana restock the pastry cabinet.

CHAPTER 15

The next day, both Chloe and Cove went to see Lottie right after church. Chloe needed to head home for Christmas once she felt secure that Lottie was doing better. Cove would head back to the shop, which was manned by all three regular employees and Melanie doing the cinnamon roll baking while Brandon managed the front of the house.

They had all worked late into the previous night getting pastries for Sunday all set up. Today, they were focused on baking the cinnamon rolls most of the town had pre-ordered for Christmas Eve, which was only couple days away.

"Lottie, you look so much better." Chloe had been really worried about her friend, but she shouldn't have. She knew that God was in control and would watch out for her sick friend.

"Chloe, aren't you supposed to be home for Christmas?" Lottie wondered if she was hallucinating.

"I decided at the last minute to leave this afternoon instead. Brandon and I wanted some time together before I left for the week." Pink tinged Chloe's cheeks as she took a seat next to her friend.

Lottie raised her brows. “Really? Time alone? Is there anything you need to tell me?”

Chloe waved her hands in front of her. “No, no. It’s nothing like that.” She looked back over her shoulder and smiled at Cove. “We actually spent most of the night at your shop.” She smirked at her friend.

“What? Is something wrong?” Lottie got a sick feeling in the pit of her stomach, and it wasn’t from the flu.

“I’d say so,” Cove said as he walked into the room.

“What? Oh, no! What happened?” Lottie sat up in bed and was about to pull the covers back.

“Whoa, it’s nothing like that.” Chloe pursed her lips and gave Cove a stern look.

“What? It was looking to be a disastrous Christmas if we didn’t step in.” Cove shrugged, and then winked at Lottie. “Everyone is going to get their cinnamon rolls thanks to your great friends and employees.”

Chloe looked sheepishly at Lottie. “I hope you don’t mind, but Cove has sorta taken over as manager of the coffee shop and authorized all your employees to work up to eight hours a day until Christmas.”

Lottie fell back in her bed and sighed. “Thank goodness. I had wondered what was going to happen.” She was already beginning to feel weak again. She had just taken a three-hour nap and woken up right before Chloe walked in. Now, she felt as though she could sleep for the rest of the week.

Noticing the bags under Lottie’s eyes and how tired she’d become, Cove felt bad for teasing her. “Hey, I’m sorry. Everything is going to be just fine. When they kick me out of here, I’ll be heading back out to the store and I’ll take care of everything.”

“My mom called and said she’s got Quinn and will keep

her until I'm all better." Lottie was grateful to her mother for her help with Quinn, but she already missed her little girl.

"Don't worry, everything is going to be just fine. I can manage the store until you're back on your feet again. Don't rush it. Take all the time you need." Cove sat on the other side of the bed and took one of Lottie's hands.

"You mean until you leave?" Lottie remembered what she'd heard about him leaving her for the rodeo. While she appreciated his help, she had to remember he was going to choose the rodeo over her and Quinn. Just like Sam did. And Sam died for his choice.

Cove furrowed his brows. "What do you mean, leave? You said something about that last night, too."

"You're leaving town to join up with the rodeo come January."

Chloe felt awkward and decided it was time for her to leave. "Ah, I gotta get going. Lottie, I'm glad you're doing better. Be sure to do everything the doctor says. And call me when you go home." She stood up.

"Thanks, Chloe. I really appreciate your help. And have a Merry Christmas."

Chloe smiled. "Merry Christmas, to you too. Oh, I almost forgot. I have your insurance card and cell phone. I also brought you the charger." She fished the items out of her bag and handed them to her friend.

"You're a lifesaver, thank you!" Lottie held the cell phone in her hand and knew she'd be able to call her mom and little girl any time she wanted now. And also be able to check on the store. However, she was tired after just a few minutes of talking; she'd probably wait until the next day to call them.

After Chloe left, Cove looked to Lottie. "Whatever you heard last night, I'm not rejoining the rodeo."

"Aren't you meeting up with Roger in January at a

rodeo?" She tried to arch a brow, but her face was too weak to move the way she wanted.

He thought back to the previous night. "How'd you know that?"

"Quinn overheard you making plans to rejoin the rodeo. I saw you had text messages from Roger you were hiding. And then a call came in that you didn't want me to overhear." Lottie did get her shoulders to move a little when she attempted a shrug. "What am I supposed to think when you're keeping secrets from me?"

"I'm not leaving you, or rejoining the rodeo. I'm meeting a friend for lunch. Someone I'm going to talk to about possible future business opportunities." Cove rubbed the back of his neck.

CHAPTER 16

Lottie wasn't sure she was hearing right. Or maybe she remembered it all wrong? She wasn't really sure what was going on. "I'm confused."

"Me, too." Cove stood up and began to pace the room.

"Are you telling me that you are *not* going to ride bulls again?" A cloudy feeling enveloped Lottie, and she worked hard to keep her eyes open. This was too important a conversation to put off for another day.

Cove sat on the edge of her bed and took her hand in his. "Lottie, I promise you. I'm not going to ride a bull ever again. And I won't be out on the circuit, either. I might train new riders, but that's all. And that's something I would do from the ranch."

Tears pricked the backs of her eyes. She hated it when she got emotional in front of men. They always got weird.

"Hey, hey now, darlin'. Everything's going to be fine. You just focus on getting some sleep and getting better. We can talk some more about this later, when you're healthy again." Cove's heart pricked with the pain he felt for making her cry. Making a woman cry was one of the worst feelings in the world. It was almost as bad as when he saw her laying in her bed super sick the other day.

Between sobs, she asked, "Are you sure you won't be leaving us?"

Cove's nose burned, and he feared he'd start crying soon himself. "Honey, I'm not going anywhere except to lunch. That's it." He pulled her to his body and held her as she cried herself to sleep. He wasn't sure how long it was, but it must have only been minutes, for her breathing had slowed and she relaxed in his arms from almost the point he began to hold her. He laid her back on her bed and looked at her.

His own tears had run down his cheeks, and he wiped them away. Then he wiped hers away and covered her up and tucked her in. Before he left, he sent her a text message saying he was going to be at the Frenchtown Roasting Company, and if she needed anything, all she had to do was call or text him.

All night long Cove kept looking at his cell phone for a message from Lottie. He did get a message from Quinn, asking about her momma. After he called and spoke to Quinn, he realized how worried the little girl was. But he did his best to calm her fears and informed her that her momma was getting better and she'd be home from the hospital soon.

"But, but, Uncle Cove, *why* can't I see my momma?" Quinn begged to visit her mom in the hospital.

"Sweetie, your momma and the doctors don't want you to get sick. Once your momma is better, you can see her." He tried to soothe her little heart.

When sniffles were all that came across the line, he offered, "How about tomorrow night I go to the hospital and we can video chat with your momma?" Cove had taken it on himself to stay at Lottie's house while she was in the hospital, so he could be close to her and the store. Mrs. Summers had agreed it was the best thing to do when they spoke earlier, but he could not, under any circumstances, stay there when she came home from the hospital.

The plan was that Cove would go over to the hospital on his lunch breaks and then again after he closed up the store. He was going to be in the coffee shop from before it opened until after it closed. Until Lottie was able to take over again, the shop would be his life. Even then, he'd probably still help out.

Quinn took in a big sniff. "Alright."

"That's my girl. I'll call you after dinner and you can FaceTime with your momma." Cove prayed that Lottie would be up for it. When he saw her earlier, she didn't stay awake very long. But another day of being in the hospital should help her out a lot.

* * *

CHRISTMAS EVE CAME, and Lottie was released from the hospital. Her dad came to get her and take her back to his house. The doctor said she was far enough along that she most likely wouldn't infect anyone else.

"Dad, can we run by the store?" Lottie had been worried about her shop, but everyone, including the doctors and nurses, assured her it was all fine.

The doctor had even stopped by one morning on his way in and picked up a coffee and scone. "See," he said, "the shop is still operating. It hasn't burnt down, the coffee tastes just as good as normal. And your peppermint scones are a huge hit. Just about everyone around me ordered one with their coffee."

Lottie had been very happy when she heard the doctor's

report. That was what helped her to focus on getting better and not stress out.

Cove had come over twice a day, and every night they FaceTimed with Quinn. Cove's reports also confirmed what the doctor had told her: her business was doing just fine.

Now it was Christmas Eve and she didn't even have all her presents wrapped and ready for under the tree.

"I think we should head over to your house first, and get everything you'll need for the next few days. Then, if you're still feeling up to it, we can stop by the shop." Her dad steered the wheelchair with her sitting in it out to where he'd parked his truck. There was an ambulance in the entrance area, so he parked off to the side.

The nurse who followed them took the wheelchair back once Lottie was in the truck and all settled.

"I still have presents to wrap. Mostly for Quinn, but I do have one for Cove and one for Mom." She felt a little guilty about the way she had handled the misunderstanding with Cove.

He had taken it all in stride and assured her that if she hadn't been so sick, she wouldn't have jumped to those conclusions. He was convinced she would have asked him about what his plans were without accusing him.

Lottie, for her part, wasn't so sure. But she kept her doubts to herself. What she wanted to do now was get through Christmas and get better so she could work in her store again and spend more time with Cove talking about his plans for the future.

When they spoke about what he wanted, she kinda agreed with him. Not that she wanted to be around bulls ever again, but he promised that he would keep them away from her and Quinn. The man did need an occupation. Especially if he was going to buy his own ranch one day. She couldn't begrudge him that.

With Cove's history of success, he would probably get quite a few young riders coming to him for training. As long as he didn't go out for long trips, she could probably get used to his job. At least, she hoped she could.

"Let's go by your house first and grab everything. Then we can head over to the coffee shop to check on your employees. I'm sure you'll see that they have everything under control. You were the one who trained them all, just keep that in mind." Her dad headed down the road to her little house, and they talked about the ranch and how Lottie's mom had decorated it for Christmas. And about how Quinn was anxious to see her.

"I've missed my little girl. I know it's only been a few days, but it feels like so much longer." Lottie sighed and watched the buildings as they passed by. Everything was all decorated for Christmas. Not a single building was without Christmas decor. Well, all but one. When they drove past the auto shop, Lottie noticed that it had zero decorations. Not even one single Christmas light, or a wreath on the door.

As they passed the place, Mr. Summers noticed it, too. "Do you think Mack will ever get over his loss?"

Lottie thought about it a moment. When she lost Sam, it took her a few years to live life normally again. While she did go about her daily living and working, she wasn't happy. It took her parents and her friends to get her to go out again, meet other people, and make new friends. Meeting Chloe really helped her. Chloe didn't know Sam and didn't know her entire life's story. It was nice having a friend who didn't look at her as though she should be pitied. Which was why Chloe quickly became her best friend.

But if she hadn't had Quinn, she most likely would have

become just as cynical and mean as Mack had. Since his wife and daughter died, he'd become the town grinch. "I think nothing will change for him until he lets God back into his heart."

"I'm sure glad you never turned your back on God. Or your family." Mr. Summers turned down her street, and they rode in silence.

But for the grace of God, Lottie might have become a grinch.

After they collected everything Lottie and Quinn would need for the next few days at her parents' ranch, Lottie and her dad drove over to the coffee shop. Cove was still there, as were Tessa and Dana. They wouldn't close the shop for another two hours, but it was busy.

"Hey there! How goes it?" Lottie looked around with a huge smile as she realized everything was still standing. In fact, it all looked really good. The only problem was that the pastry supply seemed a bit low.

A ding went off, and Dana waved before she headed to the back.

"What was that?" Lottie watched her worker leave before she greeted her boss.

Cove chuckled. "Sorry, we didn't anticipate all the people who would still want more pastries today. I think she's pulling out a tray of the peppermint scones. They're still a huge hit."

Lottie's eyes widened as she took in the people. All the tables were full, and everyone was smiling up at her. Of course the entire town knew she had been in the clinic, sick with the flu for the past few days. She heard greetings, well wishes, and shouts of Merry Christmas from everyone. She of course returned their greetings and well wishes. It was a bit overwhelming, but she felt the love of her community and cherished them all. Even Mack, when he walked in, said he was happy to see her out of the clinic and back in the shop.

When Jerod Stevens walked in, Lottie noticed Cove stiffen. She wondered what that was all about and walked over to the greet the cowboy. "Hi, Jerod. Are you all ready for Christmas with your family?"

Jerod took his hat off. "Actually, I'm stayin' in town this year. We just received our first vets a few days ago. The place where they were staying through the new year had an issue and had to close down. So the program asked if I was ready to take them early. I've been scrambling for the past week to get the ranch all decorated for Christmas."

"Oh, I wish I would have known. I'd have come out and helped." Lottie put a hand to her heart and felt the burn of tears forming in the backs of her eyes.

Jerod chuckled. "And just how would you have managed that from a hospital bed?"

When Lottie's cheeks warmed, she realized her mistake. "Yeah, I guess I was a bit overworked already. But, did you get many volunteers to help?"

"Plenty of the good people of Frenchtown came out to help me. I don't think I've ever seen a ranch so well prepared for Christmas. Somehow, everyone has a Christmas present." Jerod took in a deep breath. "I'm so humbled by all the outpouring of love and support from the entire town, and even the valley."

"Wonderful! Do you have Christmas breakfast all figured out?" Lottie hoped there were enough cinnamon rolls to give him for his new guests.

"Actually, that was what I came in here for. I heard you make the best cinnamon rolls around, and most families are able to pick up a tray here. Do you have any left?" The cowboy gave a hopeful smile and looked between Lottie and Tessa.

Lottie looked to Tessa with raised brows. "Do we have any extra?"

Tessa's crestfallen face was enough to let everyone know the truth. "I'm sorry, but we just barely made enough to cover the orders we had."

"I see. Well, do you have anything else I can buy for breakfast tomorrow?" Jerod held his hat in his hands and fidgeted with the brim.

Lottie bit her lower lip. "We could probably make a batch up and bring it over to you this evening." She turned to her father. "What do you think? Does Mom have enough ingredients for a whole tray?"

"Even if she doesn't, I'll make sure we have what you need." He gave his daughter a stern look. "But, you aren't to overdo it. Your mom and I will help, and when they're done I'll be the one to take them over to Jerod at his ranch. You'll put your feet up and watch a Christmas movie with your daughter and mom. They're both looking forward to watching *How the Grinch Stole Christmas* with you."

Jerod raised his hands. "There's no need to go out of your way for me. I know how sick you've been. I should have thought of breakfast sooner. That's my fault. I've never hosted a Christmas breakfast before. I've only ever shown up and eaten my fill of food."

The group chuckled.

"Well, around here we take care of our own, don't we, Cove?" Lottie looked to her cowboy, who was still scowling.

"Yes, we do. And I'd be happy to help out any way I can." A slow smile crept over his face, almost like the Grinch when he got a naughty idea. "How about I come over to your ranch, Lottie, after we close up? And I'll help out with making the rolls. Then I can take them over to Jerod on my way back home." Cove was going to make sure that Jerod didn't get to spend too much time with Lottie. Not while they were still up in the air.

"Then it's all settled." Lottie wondered what the look on Cove's face was all about, but didn't want to get into it here in front of Jerod. He was helping out wounded vets, and she would do whatever she could to assist him in his mission.

CHAPTER 17

What was she thinking, offering to cook up enough cinnamon rolls for eight wounded vets? Halfway through mixing the dough, she had to sit down and rest. Thankfully, her mother had taught her that particular recipe, so she took over and finished making the dough, rolling it out after it rose, and then cooking the two pans of rolls. Jerod had only asked for one, but with eight grown men, Lottie and her mom figured they'd need two pans. And they were more than happy to help.

Cove hovered over Lottie and worried about her lack of energy, but Lottie understood it. "Cove, I just spent the past few days laid up in a hospital bed sicker than I've ever been in my entire life. Of course I'm weak right now. Give me a few days and I'll be standing on my feet baking all day long, no problem." She was starting to feel better, and had offered to get up and start the icing for the rolls, but both of her parents, and Cove, all told her to sit her behind back on the chair and relax.

Once the rolls came out of the oven, Cove sniffed them and sighed. "I just love your cinnamon rolls. It's one of my family's Christmas traditions that I look forward to each year."

"Did Alice get an order for you guys tomorrow?" Lottie asked.

Cove took a drink of his coffee and smiled. "Yes, since I was working in your store I managed to get an order for two large pans. This way, we'll have plenty for breakfast the rest of the week." His grin grew, and he winked.

Lottie laughed. "Yes, you do have a sweet tooth. But something tells me with Alice's boys, you won't get them for the rest of the week. In fact, you'll be lucky if you get it for breakfast a second day." She arched a brow. If she could get up the energy to bake the day after Christmas, she would be sure to make a whole pan just for him. She'd also tell him to hide it. Surely Cove had a hiding spot for special treats at Alice's house.

Cove put his hands on his belly. "No worries, I've ensured that I have at least four put aside for me."

So he did have a secret hiding spot. Lottie hoped no one would find it.

"Cove, will you come over tomorrow night and join us for our traditional Christmas game night?" Mrs. Summers put together a night of games and snacks created from their Christmas leftovers. It was usually the Summers family and their neighbors, the Clarks. But this year they went to California to be with their kids for Christmas. She had invited the Lambtons, but they weren't sure if they were going to attend. Jessica said she would let Sarah know after their early dinner.

Cove wasn't about to let any opportunity to spend time with Lottie and Quinn escape him. "I'd love to. Thank you, Mrs. Summers."

"Please, how many times must I tell you, call me Sarah." Sarah Summers looked on Cove with love, and hoped that he and Lottie would fix whatever happened and get back on track.

"Thank you, Sarah. I'll be here tomorrow night. What time?" Cove picked up the cooling pans of cinnamon rolls and began to leave. He still had to drive forty-five minutes over to Jerod's ranch, and then another hour home to his brother's spread.

"We usually start the games at about five, and I'll have light snacks for the evening to munch on as you like. Mostly leftovers." Sara walked him out and opened the door for him.

"Thank you for helping, we really appreciate how you've stepped up this past week and been there for our girl. I don't know what we would have done if you hadn't stepped in and taken over the shop for us. And Face-Timed us each night." Mr. Summers patted Cove on the shoulder as he joined him outside.

"I'm just glad I could help Lottie and Quinn. Those two girls are everything to me, Mr. Summers." Cove set the two trays on the hood of his truck and opened up the back door of the truck's cab.

"Please, I think it's time you called me Michael. Something tells me you're going to be around here a lot moving forward." Michael chuckled and wished Cove a Merry Christmas.

The next day, after Cove's family opened all their presents, including the special gifts from Santa, they sat down for a traditional Christmas dinner with all the trimmings. Alice had gotten up early to get the fifteen-pound turkey in the oven. She stayed up and continued to baste it all morning, even while the kids opened presents.

The golden-brown and crispy skin was perfect. As were the mashed potatoes, gravy, green bean casserole, candied yams, stuffing, cranberry mold, and fried okra. Then the desserts. Cove couldn't believe how much he was able to stuff inside. He thought for sure he'd have to roll himself out of the house and down the drive to his truck so he could head over to Lottie's later on. There was no way he'd have room for anything else. Especially after he had a slice of hot apple pie a la mode.

Alice frowned. "But Cove, why didn't you eat any of my famous pumpkin mousse pie?"

Cove's eyes glazed over, and he licked his lips. "I couldn't stuff one more crumb inside. But if you save me a slice, I promise to eat it tomorrow." He grinned, thinking about his sister-in-law's blue-ribbon pie.

She chuckled. "No promises, but I'll try and hide one for you."

Cove looked at his nephews and shook a finger in their direction. "If you little rascals don't leave me one slice, I'll tell Santa to put you on the naughty list for next year."

All three boys sat up straight and gulped. The oldest, Duke Jr., said he would make sure that none of them touched their uncle's slice of pie.

Cove nodded. "Good." He turned to his brother. "And Duke, that goes for you, too."

Duke's eyes widened, and he looked the picture of innocence. "Who, me? I'd never touch your stash of extra pie, or extra cinnamon rolls." He winked at his brother.

"Why, I oughta." Cove shook his fist at his big brother. "Duke, you leave my stash alone. If you want to save some, then find your own hiding place." With a house full of men and boys, one had to hide anything they wanted to save. It was just too bad that his brother knew where he was hiding the cinnamon rolls. He might have to find another spot to hide his treasures.

"Just like when we were kids. You never could hide

anything from me." Duke laughed and patted his little brother on the back. "Don't worry, I know where to get more pie and cinnamon rolls."

"Just as long as they aren't mine." Silently, Cove was glad he had hidden his extra-special gift for Lottie somewhere totally new. He didn't want anyone to find out what he had planned.

CHAPTER 18

Quinn squealed with excitement when she ran downstairs to see the Christmas tree early Christmas morning. It was overflowing with gifts. The night before, she had asked her momma if Santa knew she was at her grammy's house, and Lottie told her that Santa always knew where the good little boys and girls spent Christmas Eve.

"Does he have a good-girl GPS?" Quinn's serious expression when she asked that question almost had Lottie laughing.

Instead, Lottie held that memory close and hoped she'd never forget how sweet and innocent her little girl was. "Something like that. But don't you worry, Santa will be delivering you your gifts here at the ranch."

Quinn ran around the tree all excited for her presents, but when her mom walked down the stairs wiping sleep from her eyes, Quinn started to pout. "I didn't get them all."

Blinking away the sleep, Lottie stopped and looked at the tree. "Honey, I think you have more gifts this year than ever. And how do you know you didn't get them all?"

"Because I asked Santa for a very special one. One that can't be wrapped up. And I don't see it here." Quinn sighed and sat down cross-legged in front of the tree.

"Are you sure it isn't in your stocking?" Lottie asked.

Quinn pursed her lips. "It totally wouldn't fit in my stocking."

Lottie stifled a laugh. While she wasn't sure what Quinn had asked Santa for, a memory tried to wiggle its way from the back of her mind to the front. She returned her daughter's pursed lips and hoped Quinn wasn't expecting what she thought the little girl had mentioned last week.

"Why don't you let me make a cup of coffee, and then you can open your stocking while we wait for Grammy and Poppy to join us?" Lottie headed toward the kitchen to make a large pot of strong coffee. She was going to need it.

"We're up," Sarah said as she walked down the stairs with her husband in tow. Everyone was wearing their special Christmas pajamas that Sarah had purchased. They'd all been opened the night before, just before bedtime. It was an annual tradition that they had done for as long as Lottie could remember.

"Thanks again, Mom. I love this year's PJs."

They all had matching red, white, and black flannel pajamas. The shirts were all long-sleeved pullovers made from a warm microfleece material. The sleeves were red, and the body of the shirt was white with a cute Christmas image on it. They all had Santa bears with a Christmas tree and presents. Michael's said *Poppa Bear*, while Sarah's said *Grammy Bear*. Lottie's said *Momma Bear*, and Quinn's said *Princess Bear*. They had been custom-ordered for the names. Usually, Sarah bought matching sets off the shelf on Black Friday. But this year she went all out, and everyone had been very excited to wear them.

Now, all Lottie wanted was a little bit of the nectar of the gods. When she began to make the coffee and saw the time, she sighed. "It's no wonder we're all so tired. It's only six in the morning." She turned her attention on her daughter.

Quinn smiled and held her stuffed reindeer closer. "I couldn't sleep." She shrugged.

Sarah hugged her little granddaughter. "It's fine. We can all take a nap later if we need to."

"I won't need one." Quinn squirmed out of her grammy's hug and stood tall. "I'm a big girl. I don't need naps."

"Well, on Christmas Day I usually do nap," Michael announced.

Sarah pulled the ham she had prepared the night before out of the fridge and set it on top of the oven. Once she had the oven pre-heated, she'd place it inside and they would have a delicious ham for their main course. It was large enough that they'd have plenty for ham sandwiches all week long.

"Can I go open my stocking now?" Quinn asked.

"Sure, I'll go get it down for you." Michael took his granddaughter by the hand and led her into the family room. "Looks like Santa left you a fully packed stocking. Does this mean you've been a good girl all year?"

Quinn sighed. "I hope so. But he didn't bring me the most important gift I wanted."

"How do you know?" Michael asked.

"Because, Cove doesn't fit in a stocking or in a box under the tree." Quinn sat on the hearth in front of the fireplace and waited for her poppy to give her the stocking.

Michael handed the stocking to Quinn and set about making a fire. "You asked Santa for Cove? Why was that? Isn't he already a part of your life?"

"But I don't want him to be my uncle, I want him to be

my daddy." The little girl held the stocking in her hand without looking inside. Her shoulders drooped and she sighed.

Quinn's admission caused him to stop what he was doing and stand up straight. "You asked Santa to make Cove your daddy?"

She nodded.

Michael scratched the side of his head. "I don't think Santa can bring little girls a daddy for Christmas."

"But it's what I wanted most. I told Santa to keep all the toys and clothes, and just give me a daddy. Then next year I wanted a baby brother." She pulled on the red ball of Rudolph's nose on her stocking until it came off. "Uh-oh. Maybe I am on the naughty list?"

Michael took a seat next to Quinn. He took the nose from her and set it aside. "Quinn, you've been a wonderful girl all year long. There are lots of present under the tree for you." He motioned toward the tree brimming with presents, mostly for her. "But didn't Santa tell you he wouldn't be able to give you a daddy for Christmas?"

Lottie was just around the corner from Quinn and her dad. She was listening to their conversation, and her heart was breaking for her little girl. All her friends, and even her parents, had told her that Quinn needed a daddy. She wasn't ready for a new relationship with just anyone. Or was she? Quinn had asked specifically for Cove, from the sounds of it. Or maybe she just expected her daddy would be Cove.

While she and Cove had gotten very close over the past few weeks, and thankfully they'd cleared up the misunderstanding from the other day, she wasn't sure a couple of kisses meant he was ready to marry her. Or that she was ready to marry him. Her attention went back to her dad when he mentioned Cove and Lottie.

"Sweetie, I hope your mommy marries Cove, too. But you have to understand, these types of relationships take time. Cove's only been home for a month." Michael rubbed his chin.

Lottie wondered if she should interrupt. But thought better of it when Quinn continued.

"But, Momma's known Cove since before I was born. We see him all the time. Why can't they get married today? I know he wants to be my daddy." Quinn set her jaw and was adamant that Cove was going to be her daddy.

"Sweetie"—Lottie entered the room to rescue her dad—"while we have known Cove for ages, it's too soon to know if he wants to be my husband."

"Oh, he does. I know he loves you." Quinn nodded and smiled.

"Well"—Lottie rubbed a hand down her face—"why don't we focus on the presents you do have here this morning? I think Santa went to a lot of trouble to make sure you had a great Christmas this year. You want to see what he brought you, don't you?"

Quinn sat there thinking for a moment, and then nodded. "Of course. I wanna open my stocking now. Is Grammy coming in to watch?"

"Right here," Quinn's grammy called out as she entered the room.

For the next two hours, they took their time opening presents and eating cinnamon rolls. Quinn had more new clothes and toys than she knew what to do with.

When Lottie opened up the gift from Quinn, she was shocked. "When did you get this for me?" She held up the matching kitchen set with the little red Christmas truck on it. It was exactly what Lottie had wanted, but never had a chance to buy for herself.

"Uncle Cove took me to the craft fair and we bought it then." Quinn giggled and sat next to her mom on the couch. "You like it, right?"

Lottie hugged her daughter. "Best. Present. Ever!"

CHAPTER 19

Cove was anxious to see his girls. He had their gifts in his truck and he was ready to go. But Alice stopped him with a hand to his arm. "Cove, you know we love Lottie and Quinn, right?"

"Yes, and they love you, too." Cove furrowed his brow, not sure where this was going.

His sister-in-law cleared her throat. "You might think you can keep secrets here on the ranch, but you can't." Pink tinged her cheeks.

"What are you talk… You saw it, didn't you?"

Alice winced. "I am the one who cleans your room."

He nodded. "Of course, I should have known. What do you think?"

"It's absolutely stunning. But, do you think today is the right day?"

"How'd you know?"

"It wasn't hard to see how nervous you were all day today." Alice smiled at Cove. "I figured you were trying to get up the nerve to ask her, and when you walked out of the house all smiles, I figured you found your courage."

"You don't think I should?" He had debated with himself if Christmas Day was the right time to ask her, but it *felt* right whenever he prayed about it.

"That's not for me to decide. I just wanted to make sure you've really considered this, and the timing. You had said the two of you argued the night she got sick." Alice didn't see it happen, but she had heard the gossip. The entire town had.

"I've been praying about it all week, and there's a peace that's settled in my soul, Alice. I do think today is the right day." Cove stopped just outside his truck and looked back at his sister. "Will you accept her into the family?"

Alice walked down the steps and stood next to Cove. "Of course I will. And so will Duke. In fact, I think my husband would dance a jig if you come home and tell him the good news."

Cove chuckled. "Yeah, he's been hoping something would tie me down here in Frenchtown for years."

"It's only because he loves you so much. And with your parents in Florida, I think he realizes how much family means to him when you're all gone." Alice's family was close by, but it wasn't the same as Duke's family being near him.

Cove hugged Alice. "Thanks. Pray she says yes tonight and doesn't make me wait for an answer. I think that would be worse than a no."

With a chuckle, Alice agreed.

During the entire ride to the Summers' ranch, Cove practiced what he'd say and when he would do it. When he stopped in front of the ranch, he said a quick prayer for strength and courage to do this. He knew this was what he wanted. He'd wanted this since he was eight years old and little Lottie Summers crashed his final fishing day of the summer with Sam.

Over the years, Cove had wondered what would have

happened if he'd been the first one to ask Lottie out. Would Sam still be here? Would he be the one who had died? Every time he thought about it, a still small voice would remind him that God was in control, and their lives, while not perfect, were what God had planned for them. Then he'd see Sam's smile in Quinn and realize he'd never wish that Sam wasn't her father. It was like keeping a little bit of his best friend with him. Which was a true gift from God.

Cove wiped the tears from his eyes and got out of the truck. He reached into the back seat of the cab and pulled out the box that held all the gifts but one. The special one was in his jacket pocket. He'd keep that hidden until the right moment.

"I was wondering how long you were going to sit out there," Michael said when he opened the door.

"Merry Christmas, Michael. I think I just needed a moment to get my thoughts in order," Cove said as he stood on the top of the steps.

"Well, are you coming in? It's cold out there." Michael stepped back and opened the door all the way. "Do you need help with anything else?"

"Nope, I think it's all in here." Cove walked through the threshold, and the scents that assailed him made him wish he hadn't eaten so much earlier. "Is that ham I smell?"

Michael laughed. "It sure is. And we have plenty of it. Come on in and set down your box and I'll help you get a plate."

"I'm not sure I've got any room yet. Alice really went all out this year. I think she thinks that by filling me up with such great food, I'll stick around." Cove chuckled and set the box down in front of the Christmas tree that still had a few presents underneath.

"Will it work?" Lottie asked when she entered the room.

Cove stood up, and a smile lit his face. "I don't I need any more enticements to stay." He looked between Lottie and Quinn, who both had on pretty red sweaters and black skirts. "I think all I need to entice me to stay is right here."

Warmth suffused Lottie's face, and Quinn ran into Cove's arms.

"Uncle Cove! Merry Christmas! I have a present under the tree for you." Her exuberance almost bowled him over.

"My little Quinnie. I have a few presents for you." He hugged her. "Do you want to unpack the box I brought and put the gifts under the tree?"

She smiled and nodded enthusiastically. "Uh-huh." She turned around to look at her mom. "Momma, can we open Uncle Cove's gifts now? Please?"

The rest of the adults looked at Quinn, and their hearts melted at the pleading expression on the little girl's face.

"Well, don't you want to play a game first? Your grammy and poppy have been looking forward to playing Monopoly with you all day." Lottie knew her daughter would want presents first, but she had to tease her.

Quinn started taking the gifts out of the box and looked at each name before placing the gift under the tree. "Nope, I want to open presents first. Don't you like presents the most? You have a present here, too." She turned around and handed a small box to her poppy.

Michael took the gift and smiled. "Thank you, Cove. You didn't have to get us anything."

"But I wanted to." Cove helped Quinn pull the rest of the gifts out and put the box to the side.

Everyone was in the room, looking at the tree and Quinn.

Cove felt a nudge in his spirit and knew this was the time to act. "Uh, I have a gift for Lottie I'd like to give her first, if you don't mind?"

Michael and Sarah looked at each other and smiled conspiratorially.

"Please." Michael took his wife's hand and led her to the couch. "Quinn, why don't you come and sit with us?"

"Actually, it's a gift for both Lottie and Quinn." Cove cleared his throat. "Would you two mind standing in front of the fireplace?"

Quinn took her mother's hand and led her to where the fire burned brightly.

"Actually, the tree might be better." Cove wiped his sweaty palms on his legs. Then he took off his jacket, but held it in his left hand. His right hand felt for the pocket that held the gift.

Cove stood a few feet in front of his ladies and cleared his throat. "Lottie, and Quinn…"

Sarah interrupted. "Oh, I want to film this. Just one second." She jumped up and went to find her cell phone. "Okay, I'm ready." She pointed the phone at the trio in front of the tree and had her video option on and recording.

Cove felt a trickle of sweat go down his temple and over the side of his face. He wiped it away and then his hand on his pants, again. He took a deep breath. "I want you to know how much you both mean to me. If it weren't for you two, I don't know if I could have survived coming home to visit these past seven years." He looked to Quinn. "Sweetie, I love you so much. You know that, right?"

Quinn nodded and squeezed her momma's hand.

"Lottie, I don't know if you ever knew, but I've been in love with you almost my entire life."

Lottie sucked in a breath and her eyes widened, but she didn't say anything.

"I remember one summer when we were eight, school was going to start the next day. You and your friends came to the creek where Sam and I loved to fish all the time. You and your friend jumped in the water and scared the fish away."

"There weren't any fish in that stream. That's why we always swam there," Lottie blurted.

Cove chuckled. "Yeah, I knew that. But it was that day I said I was gonna marry you one day. I never told Sam, but he must have known. He waited five years before he made his move on you." He shook his head and sighed. "Looking back, I see he had given me plenty of time to make my move, and since I never did, he did. He always was the one who took chances. I usually stood back and watched and only jumped in once he had."

Lottie smiled and nodded her head, too full of emotion to say anything lest she start to cry.

"Before Sam passed, he gave me his blessing. I should have done this sooner, but you had always said you'd never date a rodeo cowboy again. And you needed time to be able to grieve. I hope you don't think I'm rushing this…" Cove got down on one knee.

Quinn squealed. "Say yes!"

Sarah stifled a scream and jumped in her seat.

Michael grinned, just dying to shake Cove's hand.

Cove looked to Quinn. "Do I have your blessing?"

The little girl nodded so hard, he thought her head might come off.

Then Cove looked up to Lottie. He took the box out of his jacket and opened it up.

Lottie squealed with delight and put a hand over her mouth.

Cove took her left hand. "Charlotte Keith, I have loved you since the day you splashed around in the creek and scared off our fish. I never stopped loving you. Would you do me the honor of being my wife, and letting me be Quinn's daddy?"

Michael wiped a tear from his eye.

Sarah sniffled and wiped her nose.

Quinn jumped into Cove's arms. "Yes! Santa did bring me my gift! I knew he would."

Lottie laughed between sobs. She knelt and hugged Cove and Quinn. "I think I've loved you since that summer, too. I used to invade your creek because I wanted to see you. Yes, I'll marry you, Cove Hamilton."

Cove kissed her, and the room erupted into shouts of joy.

When he finally pulled away from Lottie, he took the three-carat, princess-cut diamond ring out of the box and placed it on her left ring finger. Then he leaned down and kissed her hand.

"Oh, I got it all on the phone." Sarah stopped the recording and put her phone down as she ran to hug her soon to be son-in-law.

"Welcome to the family, son," Michael said as he patted Cove on the back.

"Are you going to marry tomorrow? Will I get my baby brother next year?"

Lottie laughed between sobs and picked up her little girl. "I think tomorrow might be a little too soon."

"How about a New Year's wedding?" Cove asked.

CHAPTER 20

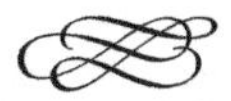

The rest of the night was spent discussing the wedding that all but Lottie wanted to take place on New Year's Eve.

"Don't you think it's too soon?" Lottie bit the inside of her cheek, worried it was moving too fast.

"I don't think it is, but if you do, then we can wait." Cove pulled her into his arms and held her. He'd wait another year it that's what it took, but he didn't think he would be able to wait much longer than that. He was ready to start his new life with Lottie and Quinn.

"Honey, why don't you sleep on it, and then tomorrow we can discuss the date more?" Sarah wanted her daughter to marry Cove right away, but she'd wait if that was what Lottie wanted.

Quinn still wanted it to happen the next day. "I don't want you to wait. I want my Christmas daddy now."

"Oh, little darlin'. I'm your daddy, even if we don't marry for a little while." Cove picked up Quinn and hugged her.

She wrapped her arms tight around his neck. "But I can't

have my little brother next Christmas if you don't marry now. Teacher said it takes nine months for the bun in the oven."

Everyone burst out laughing, and Lottie shook her head. That was her little girl. "How about we talk more about it tomorrow? I think it's your bedtime."

"Okay, Momma." Quinn kissed Cove's cheek. "Good night, Daddy."

Cove's heart expanded at least three sizes right then and there. Having his Quinnie call him Daddy, instead of Uncle Cove, just about did him in. He squeezed her tight and kissed her cheek. "Goodnight, my little girl. I'll see you tomorrow." He set her down, and Sarah took the girl to take her up to bed.

"I'll walk you out." Lottie took his hand and led him to the front porch. "Let's sit outside and talk a little bit."

"Won't you be cold?" Cove asked.

Lottie took a quilt from the chest by the front door. "This will keep me warm." She also put on her jacket.

They sat on the wooden loveseat and Lottie spread the quilt over them both.

"I understand if you want to wait." Cove did, but he didn't want to wait if Lottie was open to marrying him sooner.

"It's just all happening so fast. Give me a day or two to absorb it all, then we can talk dates?" She leaned into his warmth.

Cove put an arm around her and kissed the top of her head. "Whatever you want."

"Right now, I want a kiss. The kind you couldn't give me in front of my family." She leaned her head up so that her lips were easy for him to reach.

Cove cupped her face with his hand and looked directly into her eyes. "I love you, Lottie Keith." Then he leaned down and showed her just how much with the intensity of his kiss.

Lottie returned his love with her kiss and leaned into him even more.

Before it could go too far, Lottie pulled back and set her forehead and against his. "Wow."

"Yeah, wow is right." Cove took in several deep breaths and worked hard to control the beating of his heart. He'd never felt such an intense moment before, and he'd kissed his fair share of women. "I should probably go."

She moaned. "I guess so. Will we see you tomorrow?"

Cove pulled back and kissed her forehead. "Yes, I don't want a day to go by without us seeing each other."

A slow smile spread across Lottie's face. "I think I like that idea."

Cove couldn't help himself—he kissed her again. This time he pulled back and sighed deeply. "I better go before you dad comes out here with a shotgun."

Lottie giggled like a schoolgirl.

They stood up, and he wrapped the blanket around her shoulders. "Stay warm, and don't get sick again." He took one more quick kiss from her before he stepped down off the porch.

Lottie stood there watching him as he walked toward his truck.

Cove waved when he got inside his truck. He remembered that he'd left his Christmas presents inside the house. He was about to go back and get them, but thought if he did, he wouldn't be able to stop kissing her long enough to go inside. So he jumped into his truck and took off, watching her from his rearview mirror.

She didn't move until she could no longer see the lights from his truck.

It was probably for the best, since it was so cold outside. He had been about to ask if he could come in and kiss her some more, where it was warm. Cove knew she needed to take things slowly, as did he. But Jiminy Christmas if he didn't want to hold her and kiss her for hours on end.

But, that would have probably led to something he *knew* should not happen until their wedding night. Cove may not have been a saint, but he was going to do everything right with Lottie. She deserved to be treated special. He'd waited this long to be with her—he could wait a little while longer.

EPILOGUE

NEW YEAR'S EVE

Cove stood at the end of the aisle, waiting for the most beautiful bride in the world to walk down the aisle. All of their family and friends had made it for their last-minute wedding. Even Cove's parents flew in that morning to be there.

When the wedding march began, Cove cleared his throat and tears streamed down his eyes. He couldn't believe it had taken twenty-two years for his dream to become reality. He hoped that Sam was in heaven looking down and smiling on them. Cove had made a promise to Lottie and Quinn the day after he proposed that he'd never let them forget Sam Keith. Sam was his best friend, and Quinn's daddy. He would forever be a part of their new family.

When they said their "I do's," the entire church erupted into cheers and hoots and hollers. A cowboy wedding was always such a raucous event, even in church.

Quinn was the flower girl. Once the pastor said they were married, Quinn ran into them and asked, "Does this mean I get my baby brother next Christmas?" She patted her mom's stomach.

Everyone in the church quieted, and someone said, "Is this why you're getting married so quickly?"

Cove looked out and told the crowd it was Quinn's Christmas wish. And it took nine months for a baby, so they had three months before a baby would be created.

Santa stood up and laughed. "Ho, ho, ho. I would say March is when Lottie will have a bun in the oven. That's about when she'll need to start baking it so the baby will be born at Christmas."

The church erupted into laughs and congratulations.

And next Christmas, Quinn got her wish. A baby brother was born the day after Christmas. Lottie and Cove spent all of Christmas night in the hospital dealing with a rough labor, but when the baby was born, the entire family thanked God.

Cove leaned down and kissed the top of his wife's head. "What do you want to name our little boy?"

They had discussed several names, and if the boy had been born on December twenty-fifth, they were going to name him Christian. But since he was born the day after, he wasn't sure what his wife wanted.

"I think Jasper Christian Hamilton is a fine name." Lottie smiled down at her little bundle of joy.

"Jasper. Bringer of treasure. I love it." Cove and Lottie looked up Christmas baby names and their meanings. This was his favorite name. And he was so glad that Lottie decided to make Christian their little boy's middle name. He hoped it meant that their son would grow up strong in the Lord.

THE END

LOTTIE'S CHRISTMAS SCONES

Lottie spent a lot of time mastering her new Christmas scones. But what she ended up with was a wonderful mixture of sweet and fluffy. It's the perfect accompaniment to coffee or tea any time of the year.

If you try her recipe, be sure to let me know what you think.

RECIPE:

2 ½ C flour

1 T baking powder

¼ t salt

½ C butter (softly melted)

½ C sugar

1 egg

¼ t vanilla extract

½ C plain yogurt

¼ C Half & Half

½ C crushed peppermint (I prefer to crush candy canes myself for the freshest ingredient)*

½ C chocolate chips (you can add a smidge more if you love choc chips)

* Place small candy canes into a freezer ziploc type of bag. Put it on a cutting board and using a hammer, gently smash the pieces into little bits of crushed peppermint. I used 12 small candy canes for one recipe.

Preheat oven to 400 degrees. Combine the flour, baking powder, and salt together in a bowl. Mix semi melted butter into the flour mixture until it is evenly mixed.

In a different bowl whisk the egg, then add sugar, yogurt, and vanilla extract. Mix well. Combine the wet ingredients with the flour mixture. Then slowly mix in the half and half until you form a soft, moist dough. Mix in the crushed peppermint candies along with the chocolate chips. Place the dough on a piece of parchment paper and flatten with your hands into a rectangle. Then cut through the long length of the rectangle in the middle. From there, cut small triangles and place on a parchment lined cookie sheet, or silicon lined sheet. It should make a dozen triangle shaped scones.

Place in the oven. Bake for 9 minutes if it's a pure convection over. Or 12 – 15 minutes for a regular oven. Be sure to check regularly. The tops should be just brown and a toothpick inserted into the middle should come out clean.

Place the baked scones on a cooling rack for 30 minutes before glazing.

Glaze Recipe:

1 C powdered sugar

2 T milk

½ t peppermint extract

In a glass bowl, mix all three glaze ingredients until smooth. Using a spoon, drizzle over cooled scones. Let sit for at least 30 minutes to set the glaze.

If they aren't all gobbled up in one sitting, store for a few days in an airtight plastic or glass container.

AUTHOR'S NOTES

Thank you for reading the second book in my latest Christmas series! This year has been such a whirlwind. When I originally planned this series, it was before the Covid crisis started. I debated whether or not to have it included in this series, but instead opted for a minor mention of a super bug. I hope that did not put anyone off. It's so tough to know how much of real life to include sometimes, and how much to leave out.

I have chosen books to read/listen to this year that are uplifting and feel-good. Normally, I listen/read to all sorts of genres. But this year was different. So, the stories I wrote for the most part reflected what I wanted to read. I hope you found this series to be fun and uplifting.

My Christmas wish this year is that everyone will have a healthy, and happy, Merry Christmas and the best New Year ever! Keep an eye out next year for the next book in this series.

And if you enjoyed the world I created here in Frenchtown, Montana, keep an eye out for a short story with Jerod

Stevens as the main guy. I'm not done with his story, not by a long shot!

Also, this series is a sort of spinoff from my Triple J Ranch series. It stars Chloe Manning's family. Be sure to keep reading for an excerpt from Second Chance Ranch below.

May God bless you abundantly!

Jenna

For those of you who love social media, here are the various ways to follow or contact me:

Amazon:
https://www.amazon.com/Jenna-Hendricks/e/B083G6WQR7

BookBub:
https://www.bookbub.com/authors/jenna-hendricks

Instagram:
https://www.instagram.com/j.l.hendricks/

Twitter:
https://twitter.com/TinkFan25

Facebook:
https://www.facebook.com/people/JL-Hendricks/100011419945971

Website: https://jennahendricks.com

SNEAK PEEK

SHE WAS DESTROYED WHEN HE LEFT. HE REGRETS THE PAIN HE CAUSED. CAN GOD HELP THEM MEND THEIR BROKEN HEARTS?

Montana veterinarian Elizabeth Manning is living the life of her dreams. Dating the hottest guy in town, healing animals, and helping the homeless makes her feel she's doing God's work. So when the boy who broke her heart returns after ten years, she refuses to dig up her buried feelings.

Logan Hayes kicks himself for leaving Elizabeth so abruptly. Forced home to run his sick father's store, his passion for his old flame has never been stronger. And he's desperate to show her how he has grown to win her back.

Arguing with her boyfriend over her charitable activities, Elizabeth wonders if he's really the man God intended for her. If Logan wants to rekindle her devotion, he'll have to confess the painful truth behind his abandonment.

Will Elizabeth and Logan find their way to forgiveness and into each other's arms?

"Woohoo! Faster, faster!" Elizabeth Manning pounded her hands on the dash of Max Reinhard's Jeep 4x4 as they sped through the rolling hills around Beacon Creek.

Max laughed. "Alright, alright. I'm going as fast as is safe. I don't want to crash with you in the Jeep."

Elizabeth put her hand on his arm and squeezed. She realized she had finally found a good man.

"Ahhh!" Elizabeth grabbed the padded roll bar above the Jeep's door with her right hand and wrenched her left hand from Max's arm as she grabbed the handlebar attached to the front of the dashboard. The Jeep had just jumped a bit off the ground when Max quickly crested the small hill in front of them. Her blood was pumping, and she couldn't keep the smile from her face. It was going to be a permanent look for her if this kept up.

"Oomph." Max winced when his head hit the soft top above him. "That landing was a bit hard." He was glad he'd used the soft top instead of the hard one. Otherwise, he would most likely have a bump on his head. He certainly didn't want Elizabeth hitting her head on the fiberglass top.

Both laughed and commented on how much fun they were having riding through the country. And they were both very glad that no one had sent their cattle to this part of the region today.

They were no longer on Triple J land, which was owned by Elizabeth's family. They had instead crossed over to the neighbor's property and were about to head into Mr. Johnson's land. He raised cattle and would be rotating them between various patches of grazing land this time of year. They were four-wheeling through one of his grazing fields. It wouldn't do to drive through a patch of land where the cattle were lazily munching away on grass. They could get in the way of the Jeep or possibly cause an accident.

At the very least, seeing a Jeep jump a hill could easily cause a stampede. The last thing Elizabeth needed was Mr. Johnson calling her parents and complaining—again. Not that Elizabeth had caused a stampede. At least, not recently. But there was that one time when she and her brothers were out riding their ATVs and just happened upon a group of calves and scared them, which in turn caused an issue with their mommas. Of course, she had no idea that they were all in that part of the Johnsons' pastures. She and her brothers had spent the next two Saturday nights helping Mr. Johnson with repairs to his barn as punishment.

"Are you ready for lunch? I packed us a picnic. Just over the next hill is a nice, shady spot perfect for lunch." Max slowed up on the gas and crested the small hill.

He stopped at the top, and the sight stole Elizabeth's breath. "I'll never tire of this view."

She was glad she had decided to come home to Beacon Creek and join Milton's veterinary practice. She was afraid all the old memories of He Who Shall Not Be Named would ruin it for her. Even though they'd broken up over ten years earlier, she knew she couldn't live in the same town as him ever again. Especially the one they grew up in and had planned to come back to once they were done with college and ready to take on their dream jobs, together.

She sighed and looked out to the hills covered in tall grass and dotted with large oak trees. It was August, and the grass had already turned brown. Some blades were the color of oatmeal, and others the blond shade of wheat so common in the neighboring farms and ranches. She picked up on scents of cedar and sandalwood and knew she was home. With all the beauty of big sky country surrounding her, she knew she would have never been happy anywhere else.

The sun was at its peak and bright enough to hurt her eyes

with sunglasses on. The day was going to be a hot one, but that was only the norm for a Montana summer day. It was probably already eight-five degrees. The forecast called for low nineties, and she wanted to be inside with air conditioning once it got that hot.

Elizabeth Manning had been spoiled while she was away attending college and then veterinary school. All classes, except for the live animal labs, were held inside in nice, air-conditioned classrooms. Even some of the large barns had fans running through them to keep from getting too hot. She'd thought about having her family's farm install some of those large fans to help keep the horses cooler during the hottest time of the summer, but they couldn't afford it, yet. Maybe one day.

"Come on." Max held his hand out to help Elizabeth down from the Jeep. "Let's get the picnic set up and have some of the sweet tea your mom made for us. It's getting hot."

"I totally agree." Elizabeth took Max's hand and jumped down from her seat to the hard ground.

Even though she was tall—five feet, eight inches—it was still a jump from her seat. Max had put on huge tires and raised the jeep higher than normal. It helped when there were flash floods in the area, but it wasn't the easiest vehicle to get in and out of.

She ran a hand through her wind-blown, long auburn locks as she surveyed the land. Her blue jeans, button-up short-sleeved shirt, and boots were perfect for ranch life, and were also quite comfortable in the heat and dirt.

Elizabeth narrowed her green eyes that held flecks of golden brown here and there. Some would say her eyes were more hazel, but she always said they were green since there were only a few flecks the color of her boots in her eyes.

"Max, how'd you know old Mr. Johnson had already moved his cattle from this pasture?"

It was obvious cattle had been through here recently by the lack of tall grasses. The land looked as though someone had come through with a dull blade and hacked away at the poor grass. What had once been high grass blowing in the breeze was now chopped and not the least bit natural looking.

Cattle had definitely been feeding here, and recently, as she could still see hoof prints and horseshoe imprints in the dirt where they stood.

"Three days ago, I was at his ranch helping him order some parts for his baler. Thankfully he had most of his hay in before it started acting up. He told me he'd just finished moving the herd to the north." Max smiled at Elizabeth, and his chocolate-brown eyes sparkled like they always did when he talked about John Deere equipment. He had definitely found his passion.

Max was a John Deere salesman. He also advised ranchers and farmers when they had issues with equipment. He wasn't a repairman, per se, but he knew tractors and all the equipment any ranch could possibly need.

She chuckled and shook her head. "Boys and their toys."

He grinned. "Yes, ma'am. We love our toys big and green."

"With a bit of yellow." Elizabeth reached into the picnic basket and began pulling out the lunch her momma had packed for them once Max had smoothed out the blanket.

They enjoyed their lunch talking about everything and nothing. By the time they returned home, Elizabeth was ready to check on the mare about ready to give birth to twins. She and her boss, Milton, were taking turns checking on the poor little momma. It was her first time to foal, and she was blessed with twins.

Elizabeth was a twin, but back then her momma had already given birth to her older brother Matthew and had an idea of what to expect. *Would a young mare be ready to give birth to twins on her first pregnancy*? Elizabeth had tended to many foals, but this would be her first set of twins, and she was excited.

She grabbed a thermos full of coffee, a blanket, and the basket full of fruit and jerky her mother had prepared for her and took off for a long night of what she hoped would be helping a new momma bring her babies into the world.

When she arrived, Jewel was already lying down and breathing hard.

"Just in time. I think she's ready to deliver." Mr. Picket smiled up at Elizabeth as she entered the barn and set her basket and blanket down on the table just inside the door.

"Really? How's she doing? Any distress?" Elizabeth wore a backpack with her medical supplies packed in it. She never knew what she would need and always wanted to have her hands free, or as free as possible, so she wore a backpack instead of carrying the usual black bag the local vets preferred. Plus, with all the various pouches, she had her bag organized much better than anyone's black bag. She never needed to rummage around until she found what she wanted; she knew exactly where everything was located.

Mr. Picket took his cowboy hat off his head and swiped at the sweat across his brow. "She seems settled at the moment, but not thirty minutes ago her eyes were wide, and her head was jerking around. I was afraid she might hurt herself. If she kept it up, I was going to get one of the boys to hold her head."

Elizabeth nodded and took her backpack off. She pulled out her stethoscope and slowly walked to the horse. In a soothing voice, she let Jewel know exactly what was happening before she leaned down and rubbed the little momma's neck. "Shh, it's alright. Your babies are coming. Everything is just fine. I'm going to take a listen and make sure all heartbeats are what they should be."

She leaned down and placed the stethoscope on the mare's body and moved it around until she found the heart-beats she was looking for. Both of the foals' hearts sounded strong. Then she went searching for Jewel's heart rate. While she was listening, she noticed Jewel's water had broken.

"It's starting. If you want Becky to watch, you better get her quickly." Elizabeth knew that Mr. Picket wanted his four-teen-year-old daughter to see her horse give birth. Becky had been very excited to take part in this, and had even said she was thinking about becoming a veterinarian.

While waiting, Elizabeth collected samples from the ruptured chorioallantois in case anything went wrong with the birth so they could test it. Once she put it away, she pulled on her long gloves so she could check the placement of the foal before it began its quick journey into the world. With two foals inside this mare, it was even more important to make sure both were in the correct position.

She said a quick prayer and patted the horse's neck before reaching inside to ensure the correct placement of the little foal. All seemed fine, so she sat back and waited. There was nothing more for her to do.

"Coffee? I'm not sure how long this will take—it's my first set of twins—but coffee is always a good thing right about now. Would you care for some?" Elizabeth walked to where she'd set her thermos down and grabbed it.

"No, thanks. I already had my fair share today, ma'am." Mr. Picket tipped his hat her direction and went back to watching his little Jewel prepare to give birth.

His daughter came running in with her hair flowing

behind her and eyes wide. “Is it time? What can I do to help?”

Elizabeth and Mr. Picket both chuckled. While Elizabeth poured her coffee, Mr. Picket spoke to his daughter. “Becky, for now just stand off to the side so you can watch. If the doc needs anything, you can fetch it.”

The girl complied, but the excitement in her eyes dimmed as she slumped her shoulders and stood out of the way.

“Don’t worry, this is only the first time. I’m sure once you’ve seen a few births, your papa will allow you to help.” Elizabeth smiled at the girl, and Becky’s eyes sparkled with hope.

While Elizabeth drank her coffee, Mr. Picket moved to the horse’s head and began murmuring to her and patting her neck and stroked down the front of her head. Elizabeth realized he was worried about his mare and knew she had to do something to help him as well as his horse.

“Papa, can I come in and help calm Jewel?” Becky’s small voice showed her reverence for the occasion, but there was also a hint of wistfulness as she kept her eyes glued to the horse’s head.

“I’m sorry, Becky—we can’t have any more people inside the birthing stall than necessary. If Jewel starts to move around too much she could hurt you, or any one of us. We need to keep the area clear so we can quickly move out of the way if need be.” The vet tilted her head and wished she could allow the girl inside to help.

“Will this be your first set of twins?” Elizabeth’s voice was calm, like she was asking a normal question and had no worries in the world, even though she was worried. Although, she remembered her training and knew there was nothing to worry about. The foal was in the correct position, and she only had to wait. Normally it would be less than twenty minutes once the water broke, but with twins, things were always different.

Becky stayed quiet, but her father nodded. "Yes."

"Do you have names picked out yet?" She hoped to get them both talking and relax a little bit.

"Yes," Mr. Picket responded, while Becky continued to look on in silence.

Couldn't he do more than answer in monosyllables? It was always frustrating to get men to talk when they didn't want to. And he didn't want to. She knew, because he wouldn't look at her. He kept his attention on his horse and kept murmuring encouragement to Jewel.

When Jewel's stomach quivered, Elizabeth knew it was time.

"Alright, Mr. Picket. Please stay right where you are and don't move. Keep a hold of her head and make sure she stays down. The first foal is coming." She turned to look at the teenage girl. "Becky, you can move around outside the stall, just don't get in the way of the door. But make sure you can see from wherever you stand." With a huge smile on her face, she headed to Jewel's other end and waited for the little hooves to come out.

Once she saw the tiny hooves, Elizabeth moved closer and took hold of them and helped to get the little horse partway into the world. Once the shoulders were out, she moved back and let the little momma finish the work for herself.

Normally she would have left the stall to let the mother and babe bond and find their way on their own, but with a second foal coming, it was important to move the babe to its mother's head and make room for the second one.

"It's a girl. Congratulations, Mr. Picket, you have a brand-new filly. What's her name?" Elizabeth took her stethoscope out and listened for the heart rate, then went to the lungs. Everything seemed normal, and she smiled as she put her stethoscope around her neck.

"A filly?" He sighed and smiled. "Yes, her name is Emerald." He watched with a tear in his eye as Elizabeth moved the little filly.

While Jewel was waiting for foal number two, she licked her first baby clean and began the bonding process.

Once the second one was born, Mr. Picket whooped and hollered his excitement. Several ranch hands came over and looked over the fence of the birthing stall.

"Alright gentlemen, it looks like little Emerald has a baby brother. What name do you have for the little colt?" Elizabeth looked from Mr. Picket to the two ranch hands smiling brightly over the top of the stall.

"Jasper," Becky called out before the men could get the word out. Then they all nodded their agreement.

The vet chuckled and shook her head. "I guess you all decided together what the names would be?"

"Yes, ma'am," one of the men standing outside the stall answered. "We held a contest to see who could come up with the best names. Not too many jewel names that work well for a colt, but everyone agreed on Jasper."

"Sounds like a great name. What do you say we leave momma and her babies alone to get acquainted?" As Elizabeth stood back up, little Emerald tried to stand as well. Her legs wobbled and her front hooves crumbled in on themselves, but her second try had her standing.

"Great job, Miss Elizabeth. Thank you so much for being here and helping Jewel get through this. Everyone here really appreciates you coming by the past few nights to check in on us." Mr. Picket put his hand out, and Elizabeth took it.

"My pleasure. I'm glad I was the one here and not

Milton." She walked over to the tack room, where a small sink and faucet stood just waiting for her to clean up. She yelled over her shoulder, "Milton or I will be back tomorrow to check on the foals. Have a great night, Mr. Picket. Oh, and be sure to call me if there are any issues."

Mr. Picket raised a hand when she walked out of the tack room. "Thanks again. See you soon."

ARE you ready for Second Chance Ranch? Available in eBook, paperback, and audiobook

CPSIA information can be obtained
at www.ICGtesting.com
Printed in the USA
LVHW102344250623
750608LV00059B/318